A Light of Little Radiance

A Little of Light Radiance

by Beverley Lee &
Keith Anthony Baird

BRIGIDS GATE PRESS

BRIGIDS GATE PRESS
Overland Park, Kansas
www.brigidsgatepress.com

Printed in the United States of America

For my sister, who lost her battle with cancer this year

- Keith Anthony Baird

*For Robert Black, who was never too old to play
and who fed a little girl's imagination*

- Beverley Lee

Content Warnings

Death

Animal death

Blood (both descriptive and consumptive)

Torture

Violence and gore

Mutilation

Origins (1574)

Hoar frost brings winter's bite to the steppe. Wild things lie perished but nature bears no blame for their passing. Bitter cold preserves desiccated remains and keeps this carrion a banquet for crows. There's only bane and death here. Another storm looms in the east, beginning to fold its shroud over the jagged ridge line that punctures a rupturing sky. Soon it will rake the slopes and descend into vales with icy reach. For a lone wayfarer walking the ghost road, it spells a cruel passage through this nameless tract of the northern wastes.

It is 1574. Europe endures the scourge of witch hunts. Persecuted souls seek refuge in forgotten spaces, taking to the old lanes for safety at the edge of the civilised world. Traveller folk, already outlawed in many lands, are hunted the most because of their augury and lore. And though far from these church-sanctioned hunters, other threats abide in the shadows. Selina Dragavei is far from her kin and facing dangers not yet known. She needs shelter from the oncoming blizzard and searches frantically for a cave. But something has acquired her scent and pack underlings gather in pursuit.

Primed by the alpha, wolves close in as the first flakes of the snowstorm begin to sweep down. Selina's heart is pounding. Familiar calls are heard on the wind and she knows this heralds a wolf pack. If they encircle her on open ground she's finished, and hers will be a violent end. She makes a silent vow to cut her own throat should that happen. At full flight, she pushes hard and runs headlong into the storm. It's where there's elevation and the only possibility of finding a cave. Facing the wind, and tackling a slope, she will fast become drained by the exertion. It won't slow her pursuers. This she knows, and a waning of hope will go hand in hand with a loss of stamina.

She has a good head start but they cover ground so quickly, and unlike her, they're built for these extremes. In fur boots, and hooded deer-pelt coat, she combats the chill but moves encumbered. Supplies in a sack over her shoulder add weight but are too valuable to ditch. Snowfall begins to drive hard. In this whiteout, the chances of finding a recess in the rock face are dwindling fast. Glancing back, she catches the first of the predators clearing the scrub line, swiftly followed by the others. Frantically scanning the upper reaches, she sees what might be a point of ingress and screams her frustration and fear into the scramble for it.

Scree and older moraine litter the slope. At times, her free hand finds boulders in a part climb of the terrain. Here, the range has a shallow rise to the ridge, whereas its eastern face, though dramatic in its fall away, is locked beneath a monstrous glacier. Her pursuers are closing the distance. She hears their snarls on the wind. She ignores these promises of death and presses on. In one final push to the pitch-black artery she spied, the ground levels out to reveal a deep scar beneath a towering overhang. Never was a dark interior so welcome a sight. Exhausted, but carried by adrenalin, she wastes no time in seizing its refuge. It narrows quickly, elevates sharply, and turns almost due south as shadow engulfs her.

If she can find a nook in which to crouch or stand, her attackers will only be able to come at her one at a time. With her knife, she'll inflict enough wounds to make them reconsider their goal. It's all the chance she has. But as she turns the main deflection of the crooked channel, the dark turns to grey and then fades to white as daylight pours into what's simply a tunnel which opens up on the other side. There's the rage of the storm again beyond and the vast expanse of the glacier she'll have to traverse. She screams a 'no' and goes down on her knees. What little hope there was is forfeit, with the wolves now creeping the interior and only moments away.

It's a devastating blow. After all of that struggle, her bid for survival, the predicament is the same as if she'd stayed on the steppe. They'll encircle her here, and she'll have to make good on that silent vow. There's the briefest acceptance before a steely resolve pushes it away to see her rise and head out onto the ice giant. If they want her Romany blood they'll have to work harder for it. At this elevation, the storm is thunderous and everything is white on white. She loses her footing many times and becomes increasingly disorientated. After a while all sense of direction is lost. It's an easier route for her would-be killers. Fanning out, they do indeed surround her and the death she tried so hard to sidestep is all around.

In a bitter irony, her darkest hour has been spent surrounded by a brilliant white. A pure canvas which will make the bleed that much more vibrant. Blade in hand, she takes pause to reflect on the fact she never really stood a chance. It's been a valiant effort but now the chase is over. As the pair of wolves in front move in, instinct sees her back away, only to hear a split-second fracture of the ice before pitching over into its embrace. A thin shelf gives way and she plummets from one horror into another. Falling down a crevasse, the hell above is plucked away in an instant, only to have her at the mercy of gravity and a frozen realm.

In what seems a mere fraction of time, there's an impact. One which lances through her head and puts everything beyond the grip of consciousness. The sack on her back, the very thing she was loath to relinquish, proves her salvation in cushioning a connection with an internal ledge. Blacked out, she continues the descent in a slide down the curvature of an ice wall which deposits her at slow pace onto a rocky floor. Over a hundred feet down, she lies at the wide entrance of a cave system, encased in the stunning blue of the glacial sheet. Romany blood did indeed get spilt this day, but only the single rivulet which traces the contours of her face from the cut to her temple.

Waking brings a haze and confusion, and vision slowly shifts into focus. The sack and its half discarded contents are strewn about. There are many aches but no broken bones. She sits up, aware of the blood to her face and gingerly touches the source of it. First a wince, then a glance around at her surroundings. Now clarity. She remembers what happened and looks up to see how far she's fallen. The fact she's not badly injured is acknowledged and she's thankful. It's quite a drop and poses the next challenge in just simply staying alive. Even at this depth, there's enough light coming in via the ice fracture and its azure composition. There's even a shallow pool at the cave entrance and a narrow stream which continues on beneath the glacier. Water trickles in, everywhere.

Rising, a little unsteadily, she retrieves the sack and collects her belongings. Using a length of treated cloth, she wraps it around her blade before opening a smaller bag containing amadou, which she sprinkles liberally amongst the folds. With flint and pyrite, she brings an impromptu torch to life and takes the only route possible. The cave goes deep and descends. Though she can still see her breath, the temperature is less biting away from the ice pack and some small benefit from the flame she carries is welcome. All the while, the interior rock face expands ever outward and is soon swallowed back into darkness as the torchlight reaches its limit. This expanse is mirrored in the head room, as the space increases vertically to similar effect.

The way down is easy underfoot, with no loose fragments to negotiate. It's all polished stone and seems man-made as opposed to nature's artistry. A first clue to something yet to be revealed, it goes unnoticed in her want for escape. But then the flame begins to wash light over angular formations and the undeniable work of human hand. Roughly hewn steps are the first of these tell-tale signs. They take her down to where the floor levels out and bring a long sweep into what was clearly an early settlement. Once home to a sizeable populace, their remains lie scattered everywhere. The bones of all ages, some clearly infants, make up the large number of remnants.

What seems a central altar in a circular sanctum dominates the space. Many dead lie at the heart of it. She pauses a moment to take it in before making her way round the fallen and heading for the seat of worship. There's nothing but ancient death here and torchlight reveals five standing stones behind the altar. Clearly, all of these rectangular rocks were carved and then dragged here. Broad earthenware bowls sit either end of the horizontal piece, holding what appears to be a pitch of some kind. With her makeshift torch now faltering, she transfers the flame to the substance on a hunch. It proves a wise move, as the fuel flares into life in what she realises is a crude brazier. Lighting the other, she turns and takes in the scene depicted on the stones behind.

Now amply lit, the paintings convey meaning to what transpired here. The middle stone bears a god or entity. This bat-winged betentacled skull looms high above a hooded figure, whose arms are raised in apparent fealty. On the pair of stones either side, the masses hold aloft what appear to be human sacrifices. Selina's lore is extensive, but this is alien to her understanding. Who these people were, and what they believed is a mystery, but this place feels centuries old. Turning back to the altar, now awash with light, she sees skeletal remains laid out in its deep recess. Once cloaked, with the garment now in tatters, it seems the occupant and hooded figure depicted are one and the same. Shaman or priest is her guess, or perhaps the chief of this hideaway clan.

Pondering this, her eye is drawn to spatters of fresh blood which adorn the altar top and decorate the brilliant white bones of those around it. It's not much. Mere droplets here and there, but out of place in this archaic, dusty scene. On impulse, she checks her temple, but the blood there has congealed and so is not the source of the spill. Suddenly wary, she backs away a little and looks around.

Perhaps there's another way in? Maybe the wolves visit this place and consume some of their prey here?

As if in answer to her unspoken questions, the sound of an exhaling breath puts a shiver down her spine. The lich in the altar rattles a touch and she's rooted to the spot. Silent Romany wards against foul spirits race through her mind. After all, it has been a day of ill-omen since first light.

Moments pass. Nothing seems to happen.

Perhaps it's merely vermin in what is clearly now a crypt and not an altar? That may also explain the blood?

Calming herself with reason, she takes a step forward to peer inside. Indeed, something dark seems to shuffle a little inside the ribcage. Relieved, she leans in a touch to examine the corpse which wears winking, tempting pieces of jewellery. And then her misjudgement is met with an expulsion of sporozoa. Triggered by the warmth of her being, the thing inside the relic releases a small cloud of tiny, inky cells, sending Selina sprawling amongst the decay of the dead. Her screams fade fast as she slips into paralysis. On the floor, and horizontal, she watches in abject terror as an unearthly creature crawls out of the corpse and creeps down the side of the crypt.

Unable to move or cry out, she's transfixed by the thing that moves on webbed exoskeletal digits, with a mass of black tentacles that trail away from its skull-like form. It crawls toward her, and as she begins to drift off the last thing she sees and feels is the creature climb on top and place a slithering proboscis into her mouth and windpipe. There's a slow, pumping sensation, like a spawn being planted within, and then the blanket of sleep is peacefully pulled over.

On waking she sits up, her face free of the creature that came for her. In the wash of amber illumination, she sees it lying motionless a few feet away. Horrific and repulsive in equal measure, she shudders, reliving the ordeal, and looks up at the central stone which bears its design.

There's now a knowing imparted. Images flash through Selina's mind in quick succession. Summoned from a dark dimension, this entity of black flesh and grey bone brought the power of the void to its human host. Its great desolation can never be sated.

Selina now understands the history of this ancient site. She looks around once more at the skeletal remains of its former inhabitants. These people were its subjects. Its captives. Its slaves. Generations spent in servitude to an otherworldly master.

"What am I now?" she mutters.

The spent creature on the floor, the very same which has survived here by leaving nightly to feast on the beasts of the steppe for an aeon, has passed on its seed to a new bearer.

"I feel ice in my veins."

Her transformation is already beginning and Selina Dragavei, maiden of the wild folk, has resurrected an ancient evil in a time of holy destruction. She will leave here and drift through an arena of prey, feeding the insatiable hunger inside her, and learning to harness her new powers under a watchful moon … beneath its light of little radiance.

Chapter 1

Luxembourg, 1663 – Province of Clerveuax

There were so many people. They swarmed, in groups and in couples, ebbing and flowing like the waves of a living ocean. Flags fluttered in the early evening breeze, saffron and red and green, and everywhere the scent of roasting meat and rich, red wine.

Barsali spat on the ground like he always did at any new venue. No one paid him any attention. He was just a grizzled old man with a stooped back and a golden earring in his lobe. But Merivel knew what Barsali was doing. He was marking their territory like a dog would piss on a tree. Dusk devoured the remaining coral and gold in the sky, night waiting in the wings.

The excitement of the crowd pulsed in the air. Barsali licked his lips.

"This will do." Doval pulled on the reins, and the great cart horse stopped, its flanks heaving with exertion. It had been a long journey, but a pageant for a royal birth was not to be missed. There would be coin and drink aplenty. And, more importantly, careless people.

Easy to stash away a little for the harsh winter months. A banquet for those with a taste for blood. But a throng is a dangerous place for a vampire. Temptation burns like wildfire at every turn. They must be strong. They must be sly.

Movement in the cart. Small fingers clutched at the edge of the wooden door at the rear. A pale face with dark eyes looked out and no one watching could have said if this was a boy child or a girl.

The face disappeared and a scuffle sounded from the cart interior.

Selina banged on the side with the heel of her hand.

"Taci acum." *Hush now.*

Selina would send the children out with Lillai when the crowd reached their peak. When ale and wine had been supped and bets had been won and lost. This weekend was a time of celebration for the birth of a new royal babe. A boy born after two stillborn daughters. Speculation would be rife that this was a sign the country had been blessed, and the troupe had every intention of using this to their advantage.

Many would come and cross Selina's palm with coin, eager to see their futures. With vampires close, some of them had their futures all planned out the minute they left the tent.

A plump man waddled by, in his cups already. He barged into Selina and knocked her against the side of the cart, mumbling something incoherently, leaving a wave of wine-drenched air.

Barsali stepped down from the wagon and watched the man stagger into the crowd. Selina cupped her hand around his ear and whispered something. A smile split his face, his gums empty of many teeth. But he had those that mattered.

Lillai manoeuvred through the throng in search of water for their horse. A crimson and gold necklace gleamed at her throat, her dark hair woven into braids, tied with scarlet ribbons. Her blouse hung off her shoulders, exposing skin as pale and firm as the flesh of an apple. Heads turned to watch her. Groins grew hard.

Everyone in this small, nocturnal troupe would tear any who touched her limb from limb. She was their bait, the pretty one who lured the young men away from the crowds with a coy smile or a toss of her hair.

They all had their uses, Merivel mused. Selina Dragavei had made them all for one reason only. To blend into whatever community they found themselves in. They would pass as a generational Roma family in a heartbeat. Barsali, the elder. Selina, the one who had lost her husband to whatever reason she thought best, depending on where they were. Doval and Lillai, and the children, Morpus and Săraca. Everyone knew that Roma stayed together.

So where did that leave him, the odd man out? He knew he had charmed her that night as he wheedled his way out of a slit throat. He saw her waiting in the shadows, felt her scrutiny like hands upon his skin.

He'd been careless at the card game, his sleight of hand a little too slow. But his sweet talking had won out and the man had sheathed his blade, spat in his face and walked away.

Merivel could still remember the feeling of elation. Before he was dragged off his feet under the cart.

The exquisite pain of fangs in his throat and the dizzying draw of his blood leaving his body.

Selina's reason for making him? His skill with knives. His quick tongue.

He dragged his thoughts back into the present to find her gaze upon him. A pointed look.

"Make yourself useful."

Sometimes he wondered if she could read his mind.

It was full dark and the majority of the crowd gathered around the stage, a makeshift raised platform under the shelter of a stand of tall trees. The play had been specially commissioned by the royal household in celebration of Prince Leopold's birth.

But some still wandered around the sideshows and attractions with coin in their pockets.

Merivel watched from under the brim of his juggler's cap. This was the guise he had chosen for tonight. Easy enough to charm or play the fool, depending on the audience, leaving the others to find the stragglers and feed.

Doval appeared from behind the cart. He nodded once, curtly, a disagreement from the night before between them still needling his skin. Merivel drew his daggers from their sheath and tested the heft in his hands. He tossed a couple into the air, let one slip and the tip came down on his wrist. A sharp sting and the well of a scarlet ribbon. He brought his wrist to his lips and licked away the blood. It sang on his tongue.

Now he had the attention of the wanderers. A juggler using knives was one thing. A clumsy juggler was pure entertainment.

They flocked over to him and he gifted them with a dazzling smile.

"Gather round, good people, and I will promise you a night to remember!"

Morpus and Săraca stole across the grassland beyond the pageant like shadows over a grave. Hunger was a wild beast clawing in their guts and now it was instinct that drove them onwards. Morpus, always the more cautious of the two, dragged a few paces behind Săraca, the girl who was and wasn't his sister. One mortal birth year separated them and Morpus was the elder, but Săraca had been born to darkness first.

The sounds and scents of the celebration rolled across the pasture behind them. The roar of laughter, the sound of applause, the hot, sticky-sweet aroma of suckling pig that turned both of their bellies inside out with disgust.

And the drum of heated blood, pumped by pounding hearts. This sanguine provocation was too much for two tender darklings, especially when they had not fed for three nights.

Sometimes Selina said the others must feed them, but Săraca hated the taste of other vampire blood. *It doesn't have the fear*, she'd told Morpus when he asked about her reluctance.

"Come on," she hissed as the castle walls drew near, ever impatient with her brother. Inside were sleeping people. People who, for one reason or another, had not gone to the pageant.

A scrawny rat scurried past along the edge of the moat and she watched it for a moment, could almost taste the warm rodent blood on her tongue. But it was too meagre a meal.

The surface of the moat was an oily black, still and stinking, but they slipped into its folds without a moment's hesitation. Writhing like eels they soon found the half-submerged postern gate. The tunnel that led from it was narrow—hardly wide enough for a man—but easy access for two slender bodies.

Săraca went first, as she always did, and Morpus followed the pale soles of her feet until they reached the tunnel's end.

They wriggled out into an underground chamber filled with barrels of wine and sacks of grain. Husks clung to their feet as they padded silently to the entrance. They didn't have to look to know if anyone was there, stealing along a stone corridor with an arched ceiling and out into a wider space with circular stairs leading upwards in one corner.

They kept to the outer edge. Morpus ran his fingers along the cold stone as they climbed. Saliva drooled freely from his lips.

Footsteps sounded along the corridor above and Săraca stayed him with an outstretched hand. She knew he wouldn't be able to hold himself back. Selina had whipped their hides many times for being careless in their choice of victims.

They were hunting for a lone servant, busy about their tasks. A servant that perhaps would not be missed until morning when the Roma troupe would be far away.

The footsteps came closer. Heavy and solid. They both pressed themselves into the shadows of the staircase and watched the soldier move past, the clink of his sword against the metal buckles of his boots echoing from the stone walls.

Morpus bit the edge of his lip as the rhythmic pound of a heart passed close by. All he would have to do was … Săraca grabbed his arm and dug her fingernails hard into his flesh. His gaze fell, her arm looked strangely bare without her usual array of bracelets. But when they hunted, anything that would catch an eye or make a sound was left behind in the cart.

Once the soldier had vanished around the corner they both ran like young deer along the passageway. Lillai had said she would take them out to hunt, but she had been called to Selina's side when the royal midwife entered the tent with something bundled in a cloth in her hands.

They should have waited. But should was a word crushed to dust in their need.

The sounds of rattling pots and pans came to them on the still, stone-scented air, together with the nauseating stench of some kind of animal stew. Săraca screwed up her nose and a smile broke on Morpus's usually sombre face.

They left the kitchen behind, stealing wraithlike by the open doorway. Vampires move like shadows.

Up another staircase to a different level. Tapestries depicting hunting scenes hung on the walls. Săraca grinned. It was all too perfect.

It was Morpus who cocked his head to one side like a bird of prey and this angled her gaze upwards. She caught it a second later, the unmistakable rapid heartbeat of a child. But under that inviting rhythm was the sweet, ripe tang of fresh blood.

They exchanged a glance. The deal was made.

It did not take them long to find the room where the child slept, or rather where the child lay in bed, almost buried between two large pillows. A girl, wasted by sickness, dark circles like bruises under her eyes. Her thin arms outstretched on the coverlet were as pale as bleached bone.

A beeswax candle burned in a metal sconce close by, flickering shadows moving over the stone walls.

A stool stood by the bed with a wooden bowl upon it.

Two fat, black leeches lay in the crook of her elbows, their bodies engorged with blood.

The young vampires saw all this and dismissed it. Their focus was solely on the scent and the compulsive draw of that which gave them immortal life. Saliva pooled in their mouths, dripped down their chins. Săraca was across by the bed in a second. She snatched one of the leeches and held it dangling in her fingers. Then she opened her mouth and bit it clean in two, blood spattering onto the sheets. This was the end of the road for Morpus's hesitation. He leapt over the bed and yanked away the other leech, throwing it into a corner, and then his lips were on warm, salty skin and his tongue found the spot the leech had opened. The sweet ache of his fangs in his gums, the euphoria of hot blood coating his tongue.

Nothing else mattered.

They knew they had drunk too much but the child was young and tender and her blood came out of her like a song. When at last they raised their blood-smeared faces the child's heart had slowed to a thin whisper.

Quickly, they plucked two more leeches from the bowl and set them across their fang marks.

Morpus grabbed hold of Săraca's hand and dragged her across to the window. She was punch-drunk on their feeding frenzy, her fingers warm in his.

A gasping wheeze left the child's lungs.

This was bad. Very bad.

They had to run.

He jumped up onto the windowsill, pulling Săraca with him. A quick scan of the grassland beyond to make sure no one was watching. They descended like spiders, finding minute holes in the stones for fingers and bare toes. Into the moat they went. The water washed away any evidence on their skin, but the sin ran rampant in their veins.

"What can you tell me about this?"

The midwife made no introduction to Selina and Lillai, just laid what she was carrying down on the table by the scrying bowl.

Lillai scooped up the bowl and clutched it to her bodice. She did not know what was in the cloth but it had made her scalp tighten, and she would not risk whatever darkness it may bear corrupting the water. They were vampire, but they were also Roma, and they had a healthy respect for any forces that came from beyond.

"Well?" The midwife looked down her nose at Selina, who sat on a three-legged stool with her skirts gathered between her legs.

Two palace guards stood just outside the gaping tent flap. One had an open cut just above his eye. Lillai's gaze settled there. Selina snapped out one hand and tapped her on the hip.

Focus.

Carefully, Selina unwrapped the cloth. She knew full well what was inside it but she took her time, mainly to appear wary of the contents, but also to vex the midwife. It was a source of deep bitterness that others needed her counsel but still thought of the troupe and their heritage as dirt beneath their feet.

An amniotic sack lay within, crisp at the edges but the centre still wet with fluid.

"A caul." Selina stated the obvious. "The new royal babe?"

"Of course," snapped the midwife, but she had lost some of her arrogance, her fingers playing with a loose thread at the edge of her pale blue sleeve.

Selina drew in a breath for effect and dipped two fingers into the moist centre of the caul. She was well aware of the superstition surrounding them, that babes born this way could be special or cursed.

A slight quiver touched her. Something was wrong—but it had nothing to do with the caul.

The midwife leant forward, her mouth open slightly, her gaze fixed on Selina's face.

"This child," Selina began, "will be happy and blessed, until"—she smiled, felt the tips of her fangs against the inside of her lips—"his seventh year. Grind the caul into powder and feed it to the child, lest he fall into the hands of darkness at a later date."

It was an old Polish custom Selina had heard when she travelled through that land almost sixty years ago. She had filed it away for such an occasion as this. A dark smile threatened to curl her lips and she caught it, delighting instead at the midwife's momentary intake of breath. The stories went that babes born in cauls grow up to be vampires if this ritual isn't followed.

All lies. There was only one way to make a vampire.

The midwife nodded then scooped up the cloth. She threw three silver coins on the table and left the tent.

No word of thanks or farewell.

Selina bit the edge of one coin. It was solid. She tucked all three into the drawstring pouch she wore on her waistband.

A ruckus sounded behind the tent, Barsali's gruff voice slightly raised.

She ducked out and Lillai followed, still clutching the bowl.

Morpus and Săraca stood shivering in the shadows. One look at their faces and it was plain to see something was amiss.

Lillai placed the bowl on the ground and gathered them to her. Guilt burned a hole in her belly. She was supposed to have taken them to hunt.

Săraca raised her face. Her skin glowed with fresh blood, her lips rosy and full.

"What did you do, child?" Selina reached across and took hold of Săraca's chin. The girl's lower lip trembled but it was Morpus who spoke up.

"We went into the castle to play," he said. "We were hungry and thought we could find someone no one would miss, but then we caught the scent and"—he paused and rubbed a hand over his eyes—"she was just lying there on the bed and there was blood and leeches and ..."

"Stop!" Selina pushed Săraca away and turned to Doval who leaned against the cart, a strand of long grass between his lips. "Pack everything away. We must make haste."

She did not need to find out who the child was. One thing was certain, she was no lowly servant's offspring. And she knew the younglings had not drunk the child's death but if they had come close, if foul play was suspected, the guards would be outside the cart in a trice.

They were always the first to shoulder the blame.

Irritation tightened her jaw. She had not fed tonight and she did not take kindly to running.

Doval led the horse from the tree where it was tethered, harnessing it quickly to the cart. Merivel drifted from the dark, his knives sheathed in his hand, coins rattling in his pocket.

He raised one eyebrow and assessed the situation in a few seconds.

"Come." Selina turned on her heel and he followed, Barsali and Lillai tearing down the tent and packing away its contents. The need for blood burned along her veins. She craved torn flesh and a slowing heart held in her hands.

They crossed the grassland with the castle at their backs, passing silhouettes of cattle grazing in the dark, making for the stream which fed the moat. The sound of running water over rocks beckoned them. Perfect for washing away any remnants of the meal to come.

The stream was an educated guess for prey too. Lovers found their way here, away from the throng, lovers that perhaps should not be together. The vampires could not risk taking anyone too near the castle. Not now.

And they must be swift. They had no time to play with their food.

Quickly, they moved in the moonlight, soundless as death.

Merivel's nostrils flared. His lips parted.

There, in the clearing, half-hidden by a tumble of rocks, were two people, as naked as the day they were born. Pale skin glowed like pearls as they lay spent, the man resting on one elbow gazing at the young, shivering girl beneath him. She was barely more than a child.

Something snapped inside Selina. She clenched her teeth, raw rage simmering through her.

The man was hers.

Merivel reached for her hand and they stepped out of the shadows. The girl saw them first, her hand flying to her mouth in horror, her thoughts only of the ruin of her reputation. Her lover spun around, his hand reaching for the dagger laid upon his clothes.

He did not expect the woman to move so swiftly. He did not expect her hands around his neck to subdue his screams. And he did not expect her smile with the full moon behind her shoulder and the terrible light in her eyes.

She ripped into his jugular and that first burst of hot blood took her to the icy place of her rebirth. Merivel fed beside her, his hands wrapped in the girl's dark hair. She could hear the rhythmic sound of his suckling, could almost taste the young girl's blood on her own tongue.

They fed quickly with no mercy for their victims. There was no time to enthral. Just an urgent need.

As the sound of cart wheels rumbled on the grassland close by, Merivel took the man's dagger. He sliced into their fang marks, obliterating any signs.

Selina nodded at him as she stood, new life raging through her veins. He plunged the dagger into the man's belly, slit him hip to hip. Worms of slick, warm intestines slithered out. Merivel scooped them up against his chest and left them, still steaming, on a rock.

Blood soaked his shirt, his arms scarlet to the elbows. He plunged into the stream and washed away the evidence.

A gruff sound came from Selina's throat.

It would be a grisly discovery come the morn, but something else to occupy the palace guards and keep them from their trail.

The cart moved west in the dark, travelling along dusty tracks, through forests and across meadows. Barsali and Selina sat on the wooden board that served as a driver's seat, with Lillai and the children in the back. Merivel and Doval walked by the side, the rumble of the wooden wheels and the jingle of harness the only sounds.

Tonight they had escaped, but the carelessness of young vampires had almost cost them all dearly.

Selina watched the night sky, watched the stars scattered in the inky black.

Something hung in the air, something that began as an itch and was now more the sting of a new wound.

Something was changing in these lands.

Origins (1574)

(continued)

Selina's blood went from feeling as ice to burning like fire as she sat on that cavern floor. Something began to howl in her mind. All the nerves in her body responded to whatever was coursing through her veins. Muscles spasmed, limbs flailed, and searing pain ran through every inch of her. Amid her convulsing and changing, a hunger began to grow. A hunger unlike anything she'd ever experienced.

As pale as the glacier that entombed her, she rose with a strength her slender frame had never felt before. Her torment was gone, replaced by an awareness of nature's pulse. A newfound inner fury simmered beneath her skin. She looked around with the eyes of a predator. Her memories, still, were human. Everything that had shaped her life was still there, yet she was … evolved, a mix of the past and the new darkness that had changed her. But old ways die hard, so the crypt's occupant was relieved of his jewellery.

Attuning her senses, she felt the airflow throughout the space and followed its promise of escape. Like a lure, it drew her along the narrow artery the crypt creature had used nightly in pursuit of sustenance out on the steppe. Long did it snake and descend to the valley floor to level out and grow wider at its base. As she took a step out into the daylight, her mind was immediately flooded with fear, violent surges of it, that formed a deep subconscious impression. She stepped back before it was too late, though the parts of her that were exposed to the sun blistered and smoked.

Hastily retreating, her mind raced as she came to terms with the fact that sunlight was now her enemy. But, in the hours that passed, she discovered the ability to regenerate and heal all damage. It was a whirl of thoughts and emotions. There she stayed in the gloom, watching, waiting, until one celestial body was replaced by another, before she tentatively stepped out again and learned the moon was her ally. Now, out on the steppe, she felt the presence of all living things which prowled nocturnally in the scurry for survival. Heartbeats thrummed in her ears. Body warmth betrayed those in the drape of night as her vision could now perceive their forms. It was a new dance of the senses, and it evoked that deep-seated hunger.

By silver light she travelled. With razor fangs and enhanced speed and agility, she fed on wild blood. Ahead of each sunrise, shelter was sought in caves or beneath shadowy overhangs. And though there was still much of this territory to traverse, her return to the boundaries of the human world would come soon enough. Those who had persecuted her kind could no longer inflict their hatred upon her, for she'd create others like herself to ensure protection. There was an inner knowing that told her she'd accomplish this, though, in this moment, its full meaning couldn't be grasped. Instinctively, she knew the new shadow self within would reveal all its capabilities in time.

Until then, the predators who had chased her down had now become her entourage. The wolf pack flanked her every move and watched over her while she sheltered from the wrath of the sun. At first she assumed they merely stalked her once more, a notion which no longer brought fear as her new powerful self was undaunted by their presence. Instead, the affinity between them grew, and was as if the wolves were the first to be aware of this new connection. They were, after all, natural predators and Selina just a newborn in that sense. And so, as the nights rolled on, their bond intensified to become unbreakable, to be a pack now controlled by an undead matriarch.

Chapter 2

Muscovy, Winter, January, 1575

More than a month passed, time the shadow huntress spent learning about her new self. By the time she neared the first signs of civilisation she felt she had mastered her new abilities. One such power was her ability to walk through the freezing cold without harm. What used to be life-threatening wasn't even a nuisance to her now. But the same cold kept those in hamlets and townships close to their hearthstones in the darkest days of the season.

The first warren was nothing more than a handful of peasant homesteads. It was a dizzying experience for Selina. Their blood rapture was unlike anything she'd encountered in any hunt thus far. It called to her. Like a yearning. It was as if her new status in this world had been designed for this very harvest. She could hear their heartbeats from a distance and the lure of it was intoxicating. She began salivating. The urge to hunt, to kill, to drink, consumed her thoughts. Only a few souls braved the elements, to fetch either wood for the fire or what little they had to cook on it.

The lush satin night wore a matrix of stars that crowned a rolling countryside of snow underfoot. Each tree stood like a sleeping sentinel. A single wolf emerged into the clearing, sampling the air. The rest then stepped out of the tree line and fanned out to creep between homes. Selina followed her brood into the hamlet's heart and felt the thrum of voices beyond heavy doors. She'd had no human contact for what seemed an eternity. She listened for a while, until her hunger spoke louder than those voices.

Now it was simply about predators and prey.

Sensing something amiss in the crisp, quiet eve, a woodcutter unlatched his door and stepped out into the night. Axe in hand, he listened to sounds on the soft breeze, and knew defilers were afoot. As muscles flexed in readiness, in the tightening of hands on axe handle, her talons sped near invisible across his throat, to spray the ground on which he fell with a glistening slick in the moonlight. She came about in a swift arc, cradled his head, and put lips and tongue to his ruptured throat. It was like the finest wine: rich, heady, and a warming nectar for a core never far from frozen. She drained him quickly and completely, and hungered for more.

Two wolves nudged the slightly open door and slipped inside. Done with the woodsman, Selina picked up the axe by the handle end and dragged it behind her as she crossed the threshold. In the wash of firelight, a woman cowered with an infant in arms and a young boy at her side. The presence of the canines brought terror enough, but a vision of Hell, one clearly wearing her husband's blood, was a dread beyond reckoning. Icy grey eyes glinted at the 'food' huddled in the corner of the room and the blade was hefted clear of the floor.

Once all of the pack was inside, Selina closed the door. Why alert the rest of the village with screams from this house? At her bidding the wolves dragged the mother before her, leaving the boy with his infant sister. Selina leaned in close to the woman. With gestures, she informed the mother she must make a choice. Give herself willingly to Selina, and her children would be spared. It was harsh and cruel, but there were mouths to feed.

With a simple nod the woman acquiesced, and Selina bared her teeth, but only to issue her signal to the pack. Before their victim could scream, her throat was crushed in powerful jaws, and the rest went to work on her arms and legs. The cobbled floor turned crimson. The boy saw his mother eaten alive—just the beginning of the horror in the hamlet.

Door by door their visitation went. At each they forced entry, dispatching all in equal grim measure. It gave new meaning to the moonlit world of one Madame Dragavei, and she'd never be the same having supped from the human chalice. Now done with the feed, and warmed by its sanguinary servings, the nocturnal crew took rest in the last home they visited. Shuttering windows ahead of a perilous dawn, Selina did something she'd not done for some time. She undressed, put her head on a rustic pillow and slept in a bed.

Hours later, a small boy, bearing an infant child, emerged into the square of a nearby township and near collapsed with exhaustion. Traumatised, he'd travelled a backwoods trail away from the horror that had befallen his community. Knocking on the first door he came to, he roused its occupants. Word spread quickly and soon residents, torches in hand, began to gather in the square. A merchant, who the boy had woken, prompted him to speak.

"Tell these good folk what you told me."

Hesitant at first, the boy eventually spoke up. "My parents are dead. Everyone is dead." He went sombre for a moment, then continued. "A pale lady brought wolves to kill everyone. She is a witch."

Some among the gathered asked questions and the boy gave answers as best he could. And though clearly addled by his ordeal, his tale of wolves embellished by the addition of a beautiful destroying angel brought fear to the gathering.

It was decided a group of men would take up arms and ride north, intent on ensuring their township would not suffer the same fate.

Back at the hamlet, the wolf nearest the door became aware of distant riders and roused first. Now up and pacing, its movement lifted the rest from slumber. Selina, too, was now upright. She sensed, as they, the tremor of hoof on ground and knew it carried an enemy in number. Evasion, at this time, was the better strategy. She would harness the elements. Use that power to conceal their movement. The pack headed for the nearby hills and the caves therein, and Selina summoned the wind in their wake to fan the snowdrifts to cover their tracks. Only red death and its wreckage greeted the horsemen on arrival; its perpetrators vanished like spectres on a breeze.

Transylvania, Spring, 1575

The push for Selina's homeland saw many similar scenarios. Easy kills taken and conflicts avoided. When at last the familiar peaks of her native lands could be seen at distance, she knew everything would change. Her loyal entourage would be given up to the wilds once more. She made a silent vow to let them loose in the mountain pass, where they could establish new hunting grounds. When the time came, there was one that would not leave her side. She tried coercion, tricks, and the baring of her fangs, but nothing could dispel its steadfast loyalty.

Relenting, she allowed her single guardian to accompany her on leaving the mountains. Selina's homeland was much as she'd left it, though now under the rule of the House of Bathory. Church-driven persecution still flourished, but now it was time to get back to her people and bring her shadow gift to the Roma. Among them, she would make a coven of her own, one which would be her kin down through the ages. She'd not aged a day since her transformation—and never would.

The more time she spent in human company, the more cunning she became. Keeping to the periphery of society was after all a traveller trait, but as a darkling, it was a necessity. Feeding became an art form, with evidence disposed of in increasingly ingenious ways. She chose her blood supply carefully, but was even more particular in the making of her companions. Their mannerisms, speech, and dress made her Roma counterparts stand out to her seasoned eyes and ears, despite all attempts to hide their origins from holy inquisitors.

The first, in accordance with her long-term plan, was to be a man who would pass for her beloved, and be followed in transformation by the rest of an artificial family. The idea to create a travelling troupe of entertainers had been formulating for some time. In this guise they'd attend large gatherings, and use guile to lure victims away from the throng. And with her plan set, she set about acquiring the first of their number.

On a spring eve in a small town nestled in the foothills of the Sibiu region, Selina took to following a grifter plying his trade at cards and sleight of hand. Hooded and cloaked, she trailed him as he went from one establishment to another, extracting coin from the drunk and the stupid. He was a wily operator who also entertained onlookers with his knife skills, balancing the blade and spinning it in a well-honed routine. Physically, he was of good stock, and not at all bad on the eye. She decided he would be her everlasting consort.

His guile mirrored her own, and she liked that. At the last inn visited, his grifting went sour. A touch sloppy, his card tricks revealed his cheating ways and almost earned him cold steel on flesh. After a heated exchange, he made haste and caught sight of her, and felt a lure so intense he'd later swear it had been deviltry. Like a moth to a flame, he was hers, dragged beneath a cart standing in the shadows of a stable's side awning. She transformed him right there, wrapped in her cloak, with her mind demanding his name in that moment: Merivel, came the answer.

It took Merivel many days and many questions to come to terms with his new form, though he was enchanted with Selina. Her long, fiery locks, slender figure, and ice-grey eyes were the personification of the darkness that had claimed his inner throne. He would follow her to whatever end and think nothing of the cost. He needed training and so she took him off the beaten track to woodlands. His first feeds would be deer and the wagon Selina had stolen would provide cover by day. Besides, whispers of inquisitors were rife, and so she'd found a spot by the river to make a camp, putting them far from prying eyes. On the second night, under the stars, Merivel received the first of his new life instructions.

"How do you feel?" she asked

"More alive than I've ever felt … in the strangest of ways … and yet endlessly empty," he said.

They studied the constellations, in a firmament more vivid than either had ever seen with former eyes.

"The emptiness will only ever be quenched at feeding. It brings a measure of comfort, which slowly creeps away, only to have that feeling return."

He turned from the heavens to her. Studied her fine features, and then replied. "You devoured my blood. I understand this is how I must feed if I am to exist this way. So, in fact, we are killers, no?"

She dropped her head and sighed. "I've given you the gift. How you use it is up to you. You can live on the blood of animals from this day forward. I care not. But know this, you'll be driven by your urges around people. If you choose to abstain, I believe it will drive you mad."

Pausing, she turned and looked him in the eye. "Human blood is like nectar. Once tasted, all else pales against it."

He pondered her proclamation. "When do I get to dine?" he asked.

"Oh," she said, and looked into the tree line. "I'm sure the answer to that lies in your willingness. After all, this place is alive with the creatures of the night."

She turned to her grey guardian, Lodai. "Isn't that so, my loyal friend?"

Lodai lifted his head off the ground and cocked it to one side. Selina flashed Merivel a look which promised adventure and thrilling encounters. But for now, the hunt and his training was all that mattered. She took him in search of deer and ensured they'd be sated long before morning, wasting no time in orchestrating his bloody baptism.

Selina's lessons seemed endless. At times, Merivel would lose patience, but she always remained calm at his protests. It was no small thing to be born to darkness, so she allowed him space to come to an acceptance. It wasn't long before they were discussing the finer detail of the 'family' they would create.

"Is it right to turn children into what we are?" he asked, one night whilst travelling.

Before she could answer, it inspired another question.

"I don't even know what we are. Do you?"

Selina answered the second first. "We are the children of an elder god, forgotten."

Contemplation stole her away, momentarily.

"Perhaps we are something of folklore and myth. Who can tell? All I know is we sit below that god but above men."

Her answers were punctuated by the rattle of the wagon and the clatter of hooves.

"As for children. Is it not widely known that in the seizing of lands men have had them thrown from city walls? Burned at the stake or gutted like pigs in front of their mothers? And did not the Northmen of old throw infants into pits of wolves for sport?"

She let the words hang before continuing. "We might steal their innocence, but we do not exploit it for gain or barbaric entertainment."

As soon as Merivel was accustomed to his new state, and all questions given due weight and consideration, they set about making the rest of their Roma brethren. It was a time of wild excitement. They chose an elder, a brother for Merivel, and for Selina a sister who would have children of her own: two, whose father would have died in some fictitious way. With a plan in hand, they kept careful watch wherever they roamed to fulfil their endeavour.

Soon, a maiden named Lillai fell for Merivel's charms and followed him into a copse of trees on the promise of a lustful encounter, only to receive an altogether different kind of penetration. By a similar premise, Selina lured a man called Doval to his fate. Days later, traversing a secluded vale, they encountered an exhausted old man at dusk.

Having taken a late afternoon stroll by the river, he was resting up on a rock with his sore feet in bubbling water, only to fall foul of wandering fury. And of the children, Săraca, having spent too long collecting wild flowers and straying from familiar paths, had gotten lost in the failing light and met the purveyors of her new destiny in the wilds.

Nearly a month later, a boy called Morpus came to darkness himself, as a child stepping from the daylight for the last time by wandering the moor far too late and meeting 'the Devil' at a lonely crossroads.

Selina Dragavei's new brood was now complete. When all were well versed in their new powers, they assumed the guise of the entertainers Selina had foreseen and set about their nocturnal activities—so many warm bodies to be delirious among, so much crimson cream to taste …

Chapter 3

The Forests of Prussia - 1704

The stench of rotting flesh drew the wagon onward. Winter howled at their backs, the heavy snow making the journey slow and tedious. Moonlight speared through the bare canopies of the trees and no mortal risked life and limb in such treacherous conditions.

Difficult times for a small troupe of vampires who could not dwell in the same place for long. Merivel walked ahead, a staff fashioned from a stout oak branch in his hand. It did not tire him to walk through the deep snow but their horse was close to exhaustion and he swept as much of it from their path as he could.

Morpus sobbed in the back of the wagon, hunger wracking his small frame. They were deep into the dark forests of Prussia now, Selina taking her band out of densely populated areas.

Because they would be targets.

Fear of witchcraft ran like the plague throughout all of Europe. Men, women, and children all tortured and hanged, or burned or drowned. It need not matter how they died, as long as they did.

But now they were starving and animal blood had ceased to provide enough nourishment.

Barsali snapped the reins over the horse's back, his mouth set in a thin line. "I don't like the feel of this place."

The stench grew stronger as they rounded the bend in the forest track. A valley lay before them, a small village nestling at its base. The road leading to the village was flanked by a line of trees.

From each of these trees hung a corpse, some plucked to bone, some fresh enough to turn a small vampire's head. Lillai pulled Morpus closer as the wagon lurched past. His fingers clutched the wagon side. They could not feed from the dead.

The ropes that held these unfortunates creaked in the night breeze.

As they passed the last tree, the falling sound of something wet and glutinous made them all turn, saliva pooling in their mouths. A heap of cold entrails glistened on the snow. The freshest corpse, its belly slit, possibly hung there that day.

It was a warning that witches were not tolerated.

"We can be in and out in minutes," Merivel said, his eyes tracking over the huddle of rooftops below.

"That might ring true, but we cannot afford to be dressed in their crimson. The snow will scream our guilt."

Selina patted Doval on the arm. There was no love lost between him and Merivel, but this time he was right. She knew that they were too alike, that they saw their own weaknesses reflected in each other.

"No," she said, her hand resting on the heaving flank of their horse. "She needs food and rest or we'll be pulling this wagon ourselves. We go into the village, say our children are starving, say we are fleeing from the band that torched our hamlet."

They all had seen the smoke from such, writhing into the air, smelled the stench of roasting flesh, had lamented the waste of so much blood.

"We go to the inn," Selina said. "From there we can choose our prey."

Barsali clicked his tongue but the horse didn't move. Her head hung low, her nostrils flaring, breath escaping in ghost clouds.

Săraca jumped down from the wagon. She slipped a slim hand into Selina's, looked up at her maker's face.

The girl knew before it happened.

The horse's knees buckled and she fell onto them. A moment where she tried to stand and then the effort became too much. The sound of heavy flesh meeting snow, the shivering of skin and the wide-eyed fear.

She knew too.

Merivel drew his dagger. Săraca was on her knees in an instant, her hand stroking the horse's muzzle, cooing gently as if she was calming an infant. Merivel sliced through the flesh above the jugular, and parted the skin. The thick vein of life lay below. Blood dribbled onto the virgin snow. He worked quickly, aware the horse was still conscious. She had served them well. He pulled Săraca's hair out of the way as she lowered her head, as Morpus appeared beside her.

They let the children feed but knew it wouldn't sate their appetite for long. Barsali jumped from the wagon and began to unfasten the harness. The bit jangled in his hands as he pulled it from the horse's foam-flecked mouth. He went around the back of the wagon and stashed the harness away.

Selina met him as he jumped down.

"It's an ill omen," he said. "We need to move on."

Selina placed her palm against his stubbled cheek. "Omens don't fill our bellies."

He grunted. Selina knew he didn't like it but he would follow her. They all would.

Their parting gift was to the wolf. After the children had drunk their fill, Doval slit the horse from shoulder to groin. Viscera steamed for only moments before the wind snatched the warmth. But the wolf would find it. He didn't need his food hot.

With the wagon dragged off the track and hidden under fans of pine, the troupe made their way on foot to the village.

At the end of the main street golden lights spilled out onto the snow. Doval raised his head and sniffed the air.

"It stinks of meat," he said. He wasn't talking about any beast in a cooking pot, he was talking about people. Doval was the one who had lost all shreds of his humanity. Humans were a food source and nothing more.

"Take the children around the back of the inn," Selina said to Lillai. "Barsali, you go with them."

Too many strangers at once would raise suspicion, as would a single woman.

Merivel opened the inn door, with Selina and Doval at his heels. If they had been human it would have been the warmth from the fireplace that drew them close, but the only warmth vampires crave is from an opened vein.

A few men cast a glance in their direction.

Selina pulled her shawl around her shoulders and lowered her head demurely, keeping behind Doval as Merivel went to the bar. He tossed a coin to the innkeeper and settled himself on a stool. The innkeeper drew a flagon of ale and pushed it across the bar.

"You have a problem with witches," Merivel said, catching the man's eye and holding him in his gaze. "We saw the bodies as we came down the hill."

"We've been overrun by the damned," the innkeeper said. "Young girls frolicking naked in the fields with beasts.

Good crops dying overnight. It can be nothing else but witches. We do what we must to purge them."

Merivel nodded as he raised the flagon to his lips in pretence. He could hear the blood pumping through the innkeeper's heart, wanted nothing more than to yank him across the bar and sink his fangs into an artery. He glanced across to Selina, saw her eyes flicking around the crowded space. Looking for victims. Doval had gone into another room at the back of the inn, checking for another escape route. They may be vampire but they were vastly outnumbered in this place.

A shout came from the back room, a man's voice raised in anger. Sounds of a scuffle. The crack of a stool thrown against a wall.

Merivel made his way over to Selina. "Feeling runs high here. They are nervous and volatile. We must be careful."

It was not ideal. But they had to feed. They did not have a choice.

Morpus appeared at the window, a pale wraith against the night. He was alone. Selina slipped out and took his face between her hands. "Where are the others?"

Morpus opened his mouth to speak but his words died on his tongue. She could smell fresh blood on his breath.

Somewhere in the dark, a lone wolf howled.

"Where?" Selina shook his shoulders, roughly.

"Guards," Morpus finally said. "'They were patrolling, searching the alleyways. I think they heard me feeding. Lillai pushed Săraca behind a water trough. Then Lillai knocked over a bucket so the men would look at her …" The boy paused and tears welled in his eyes.

Selina did not need to hear anymore. Merivel's words echoed in her head. The people here were looking for scapegoats. And they had bloodlust running in their veins. Her little troupe had wandered into a powder keg awaiting a spark.

Barsali scrambled across the top of the wall that joined the circular tower at the edge of the village. From here he had a bird's eye view of the men, eight in total, walking with their torches held high, flames licking at the night.

Lillai walked between them, her arms held by two of the men. Barsali could smell the lust upon them. His fingers trembled. He wanted to tear them limb from limb.

Lillai was strong and could probably take down four of the men, but not eight. Two carried long pikes, the wicked blade at the top glinting in the torch light. That blade could open a belly in seconds.

He ground his back teeth together and chastised himself for leaving Lillai and the children alone to follow a scent into a back street which had led to a bolted door. Barsali hadn't wanted to come here. He preferred solitary dwellings, in the middle of nowhere. Some place where the inhabitants could be dragged out and fed from, where their screams and pleas didn't matter. He loathed careful stalking and quiet kills.

The guards arrived at the tower door. One banged on it with his fist, and it opened.

Lillai raised her face and met Barsali's eyes for a moment. She knew what awaited her inside.

But Barsali knew her fear was down to a single fact. All too soon the sun would rise over the mountains and nothing could save her if its light touched her skin.

The vampire troupe gathered in the shadow of the tower's side. Morpus and Săraca clung to each other, their eyes roaming over the stone walls. Imagining what was inside.

Selina took a few seconds to allow regret for her decision to come here to settle, then she scraped that regret away. Lillai was blood kin. She would not let her fate be decided by men.

A plan was forming in her mind. She licked her lips, her eyes dark below hooded lids.

"Morpus." Selina called the boy to her side. "You will go and buy ale at the inn. Tell them it's for the witch hunters in the tower, they have a new she-devil." She motioned for Doval to follow him. "Take Săraca, but let Morpus enter alone. A boy child will go unnoticed."

Selina let her gaze fall on the tower. She looked at it from base to tip. It reeked of death. Reeked of pain. A torture chamber for those accused of witchcraft, and now a vampire was imprisoned there. It wasn't as if blood drinkers were an unknown source in these times, but people would rather blame innocent young women than see the true devils that walked among them.

"Merivel." He came to her, his jaw set tight. "Find another entrance. There must be one. When you hear Morpus return …" He nodded before she had finished her sentence and melted into the dark.

She turned to Barsali. "Wait here, and keep the men occupied. Hold them at the door for as long as you can. Play the pleading grandfather. Use what you have. You will get your chance for blood."

Barsali wanted to follow Merivel, to force his way into the tower and spray scarlet upon its walls. But he trusted Selina's plan more than his own needs.

Doval drifted out of the alleyway with Morpus at his side, both carrying steins of ale. Doval set his down by the door. Selina motioned for him to go around the back of the tower. She pressed her spine into the wall where the shadows grew deep.

Morpus knocked on the door, his chin raised in defiance, his courage a blanket around him. A man in a leather apron opened the door. Laughed as Morpus offered the ale. A guard appeared and they shared a joke. The man with the apron ruffled Morpus's hair and tossed him a coin. One thing Selina knew about torture was that it was thirsty work.

She crept through the wall's shadow towards the rear of the tower. The sound of crumbling stone reached her ears.

A small window stood open to the night, the metal bars that had crossed it bent out of shape and sticking from the wall like burnt bones. She scrambled up, spider like, and eased herself in through the hole.

It smelled like death here. Not new death, like the kind they left after feeding, but old death that lingered long after the corpse had gone. Rats ran through filthy straw, scurrying for cover in the blackness. The vermin knew what walked amongst them now.

Merivel and Doval stood at the end of a line of empty cells. The air reeked of human waste and desperation. Those who had occupied these cells now hung on the trees on the hill for all to see. It was little wonder the men had targeted Lillai. She was young and female and not from these parts. Enough for them to brand her witch.

Faint flickering light came from a room at the end of a narrow corridor. The squeal of a wheel turning, the creak of a rope. A voice pleading.

Merivel crept to the doorway.

A young man lay strapped to a rack, his arms and legs bound by rope, his naked body gleaming with sweat and blood.

Two guards sat in the corner playing cards on an upturned ale barrel.

"Confess," said the torturer with his hands on the rack wheel, leaning over so his face was inches from his victim. "You harboured the witch." He notched it on. Merivel saw a tendon snap under the prisoner's skin, smelled the heat of his blood as he cried out. His mouth watered.

He made his decision. Doval and Selina were behind him. They were no longer outnumbered. And the stone walls of this place were made for silencing screams. They would dispatch their own justice.

He stepped out from the shadows like a phantom from a grave. The man by the rack reached for a dagger in his belt. But his fingers never touched it. Merivel was upon him in an instant. They fell against the barrel, the two guards thrown to the side. Merivel grasped the man by the throat, dragging him across the filthy floor, his legs kicking uselessly.

Doval and Selina moved as one, ramming the other men against the wall. Doval leaned in, opening his mouth, letting his fangs glisten.

"Witches are not what you should fear," he said. He grabbed the knife from his quarry's boot, examined the blade in the guttering torchlight, then plunged it through one of the man's eyes, pinning his head to the wall. Warm blood spurted onto Doval's face and he grinned, licking it from his lips before his fangs found the carotid artery in the quaking throat.

Selina let her victim watch, his fear seasoning her hunger.

Merivel yanked his meal towards the shackles hanging from the ceiling. He snapped them around the man's wrists, pulling him closer by the throat.

"Where is she?" he said, through gritted teeth, because it was obvious to them all that Lillai was not here. But the man was beyond panic and could not form a single word.

Frustration combed through Merivel's veins. He drove his fist into the man's mouth, shattering teeth into the dirt. Blood spattered his face. He leant in, placed his mouth over the ruin and suckled like a newborn. His fangs closed over a trembling tongue. He ripped through it, severing it as its base, spitting it out on the floor. A throat tried to scream but it was drowning in its own blood.

The stench of human waste filled the cold air. Selina allowed the anger that was bubbling under her skin to surface. She let it fly, straddling the quaking mass at her feet, her fangs shredding his throat in seconds. She drank, deeply, knowing the pain this caused. He deserved nothing less.

Merivel spat out what remained of a lip, ripped away a filthy shirt and sank his fangs into his prey's chest, above his heart space, his preferred method when he knew he would not be disturbed.

For a few minutes the only sounds were of suckling and pain-drenched moans that faded to nothing. Blood dripped from the dungeon walls, pooled on the stone slabs beneath their feet. The vampires lapped at their victims until their bellies were full.

Merivel wiped his face with his arm, white fangs glistening through the smeared crimson. There was no sound from above and Selina grunted with satisfaction. Barsali had done his worst.

But now her thoughts turned to Lillai.

She backtracked to the cells, kicking open the doors, but her acute sense of smell could detect nothing that spoke of Lillai.

"Did she break free?" Doval asked, leaning against the bars beside her.

"If she did, there would have been nothing for us to feast upon," Selina said.

"Agreed." Merivel added his affirmation and Doval shot a black glance in his direction.

"It may not be long before others come here. We do not know their routines. Let us barricade the door from inside and stay the window. It may give us valuable time as we search."

Selina knew that once what they had left was discovered, the townsfolk would be hunting more than supposed witches.

Doval ran up the winding steps leading to the tower door. He did not ask for Merivel's help.

Merivel followed Selina to the window, but not before he snapped the neck of the poor soul upon the rack. As she inched her way through, with the grace of a black widow spider, she turned to him. "You should not vex Doval. He is your brother in blood and we need to be as one."

Merivel felt the heat from his meal rush to his face as he edged through the window. She had gone on ahead, not waiting for him. He clung to the wall and bent the bars back into place, her chastisement ringing in his ears.

Lillai held the man's face between her palms. He was young, not long from boyhood, with a scruff of beard upon his chin. Erik was his name, drawn out of him in passion.

It had been easy to charm him with a promise as he took her down into the cells. She was proficient in the art of doe-like eyes and glances from under thick, black lashes. Easy to press herself against him and plead. The promise to lay with him would be more than he could resist.

He led her down into a chamber below the cells. A chamber that opened to an underground tunnel, and the outside world. Flesh has its uses and she was queen of persuasion, taught by Selina and honed over the decades to an art form.

She looked deep into Erik's blue eyes, stroked her fingers across his cheek. In another time she may have even loved him. His features pleased her.

"This was how it was meant to be," she whispered, placing a kiss upon his brow. "But I'm going now. You can watch me if you'd like."

Blood dripped down her arms, her bare feet standing in a dark, spreading puddle. She walked to the door. Moonlight streamed through a gap in the wooden slats. Lillai raised her hands and drove Erik's head onto the pike he had so proudly carried.

Barsali stood in the village square, his clothes blood-soaked, his belly full. He stared down the barrels of a dozen rifles and too many pistols to count.

Rage made his fists clench. Rage with a spread of self-rebuke.

He had made short work of the man in the leather apron and the one with the cocky smile. Had held that one down as Morpus fed. Instructed the boy on the most tender spots, pulled his head away as the heart stuttered to a halt.

Barsali had been sure no one watched them, but someone *had*. Maybe from a crack in a shuttered window or from a deep shadow overlooking the tower door.

And now they had him cornered. He could force his way through but knew that a hail of bullets would slow him enough for them to be on him in an instant. Did they know what he was? Fear of witchcraft seemed to rule their actions but did that run to vampires too? All they had to do was keep him out here until the first rays of the sun spread across the rooftops to discover his truth.

But maybe if their attention was all on him, it would give the others a chance to escape. Thank the blood gods that Morpus had slunk away after feeding, in search of his sister, both as slippery as eels.

The tip of a long pike poked him between the shoulder blades and he spun, keeping his fangs hidden even though they ached in his jaw.

"What are you?" a voice called out from the crowd.

"Witch!" someone shouted.

"Burn him!" called another.

"Find the strangers and burn them too. They bring death here. They are devils!"

Barsali looked up at the sky, calculated how many hours of darkness were left. The stars were beginning to fade. His gaze flicked into the deep shadows of the overhanging rooftops.

The others were there. He could feel them. This could soon become a bloodbath, but they would not all survive. And Selina never took too deep a risk. If he was her he would have slipped away and left him to his fate. He wanted her to do that.

But he didn't want to die. She had given him a new life when his own was close to its end, and he had easily come to terms with killing as a means to live. In truth, he loved this life more than his mortal one.

The crowd closed in. Barsali could smell their fear even as they held their weapons high. A shot rang out. He felt the air shift as the bullet swept past his ear, hissed at the harsh sting as it burned the lobe. His nostrils flared. *So be it.* He would take as many down as he could before they filled his flesh with holes.

A flicker of something gold down an alleyway. It drew the attention of the people milling at the back of the crowd. Smoke wafted over a rooftop, followed by a finger of bright flame.

"Fire!" The shout rang out into the dark.

The flames leapt to another rooftop, licking down walls, eagerly devouring timber-clad frames. Somewhere close, hoofbeats rang out on the cobbles.

The crowd backed away, now caught in another dilemma. The houses here were packed together. Fire would claim a whole street if left untended.

A stiff breeze stirred the flames higher, scattering sparks into the night, giving them wings to reach yet another rooftop. The sound of one collapsing, the groan of old timber.

People ran for buckets. Cries to bring water from the river.

Barsali was left in a ring of around a dozen men. They exchanged glances. Two drew swords. One cocked a musket, his finger on the trigger.

They were past the need for any kind of trial, if indeed that had ever been on their minds.

"What sorcery is this that you bring fire?"

Barsali shook his head. "You think me responsible when I stand before you?"

"You called upon the Devil's aid!"

Go, Selina. He urged her silently. *This is your chance.*

Now the hoofbeats echoed around the town square. Heads turned. Smoke drifted thickly from the alley's mouth.

And then, through the smoke and the flames licking across from rooftop to rooftop, two horses burst through, a grey and a black, two small forms clinging to each back, their fingers wound into manes, their heels against the horses' flanks. Behind them, on ropes tied to halters, were two other horses, these with feathered feet. One reared as it skidded on the cobbles, the whites of its eyes gleaming in the dark.

Everything was chaos and noise and flame.

Morpus dug his heels deeper and his mount raced into the crowd, scattering those who did not jump out of the way. The horse, driven half-crazed by fear, ploughed through the men surrounding Barsali. One was trampled, his bones splintering as hooves smashed into his flesh.

"Come!" Morpus held out one hand. Barsali took it and leapt up behind the young boy. The horse needed no urging to make haste in its escape from the rapidly spreading fire.

They caught up to Săraca, Lillai pressed behind her, her skirts covering the horse's back. Hooves flicked up clods of snow and earth as four shapes galloped up the slope leading from the village. Selina with Merivel, Doval on his own, all bent low on the horses' necks, urging them faster.

The troupe did not fear the chase. They feared the creeping dawn they all could feel over the mountain range.

At the top of the slope they pulled up for a few seconds and watched the village below them burn to the ground.

Morpus leant across and slapped his palm against Săraca's. Grins on two filthy smoke-stained faces.

They raced on with the dawn at their heels, the children falling asleep even as the others leapt from their mounts and staggered into a deserted church. Merivel had the presence of mind to pull his horse with him.

The first rays of sunlight burst through a broken stained glass window as the vampire troupe crawled into the crypt and fell into their dreamless sleep ... all save Selina, who was visited once again by the recurring nightmare which had haunted her since that fateful day on the glacier.

Chapter 4

Five Days After the Blaze

Desider von Brandenburg dismounted from his horse and surveyed the ruin of the village. He took a deep draw on the air which was heavy with decay and bitterly cold. Pondering something, he instructed his men.

"Gather the bodies. They shall be burnt, but first I must inspect each one."

Now mid-fifties, he'd served the Holy Roman Empire for three decades as a hunter of those bound to darkness. His legacy of destruction under the banner of righteousness was legendary. Latter years had brought a new evil to his attention, one which bore a distinctive mark of the Devil. Telltale puncture wounds had him on the trail of these agents of the unearthly and this nameless place was but a mere stop upon that quest.

With all corpses gathered, an undertaking which had lasted most of the morning, he began the grim task of examination. By noon it was clear those he'd been following were indeed the maleficarum who had perpetrated this unholy atrocity. The same hallmarks of their feasting had left a bloody trail across the land. Countless testimonies from God-fearing souls had built up a picture of their activities, granting the witchfinder evidence enough to fill an ever-growing treatise on the subject of vampirism. One day it would find its way to Rome and form the foundation of a papal bull concerning all manner of deviltry, but for now it was his armour against dark forces.

A lone crow came to gaze upon the human remains. It perched on the charred awning of the razed inn and cawed at Brandenburg's crew, as if in thanks for laying out such delicious fare. The witchfinder took a moment to study the bird. He wondered what master it answered to. *Was it the Divine or the one cast out and made low?* Either way, the creature and its brethren would dine no longer on the wretched of this place as he ordered all victims be doused with pitch and put to flame. As black smoke rose once more from the shell of the village, Brandenburg's seasoned trackers led the horsemen to the outskirts and beyond, eventually coming to the site of an abandoned church.

All evidence pointed to a place of respite for their quarry, but the hunters knew they'd long since departed. They'd overnight in this forgotten House of God, rest their horses for a good spell and redouble their efforts by riding long and hard in the coming days. The trackers estimated no more than a week had elapsed since the visitation by those they sought. There was snow on the ground, more threatening to fall, and the only way out of the vale was up and over the mountain range. They would now be at high elevation and conditions there would be more extreme. It would slow the perpetrators down and give Brandenburg's band of hunters a chance to close the distance between them. Desider knelt down in the crypt, took up a handful of dirt, and let it cascade through his fingers.

"You come and go as dust on the breeze … feeding your un-death in the dark. But this servant of God sees you, knows you, and will smite thee with the wrath of Heaven," he whispered.

The mountain pass was treacherous. Unused for decades, it was a broken road strewn with the debris of rockslides and storm-fallen trees. Coupled with snow, tracts of ice, and merciless wind, the way through the range made progress a slow affair. At times unsure of their footing, horses were spooked and harder to control on lethal ledges. Only Selina's tenacity and experience kept them on course for an exit from these unforgiving mountains. In a blizzard, they holed up in caves to wait out the worst of it and shelter from cruel daylight. Their recent human harvest would sustain them long enough to be clear of the high ground, though she foresaw the inevitable sacrifice of a few steeds along the way.

In undead slumber, they took to the void of stasis, except for Selina who was visited once again by the thing she deemed her 'endless nightmare' …

A black heart lies torn from the chest of a shrouded figure. It bleeds out onto cold earth, the last of the blood which has sustained its host for centuries. In accelerated decay it degrades to dust and is carried from the scene by an ethereal breeze. Riders, hooded and cloaked, are but black figures of death against the raging sun on the horizon.

On a broken bough a lone raven sheds a single tear. It mourns her loss. It knows her horror.

The silver crucifix, suspended from a chain, glints as it catches killer rays of light before falling into the litter of once immortal bones. There, it nestles among bleached shards as a commanding ward to the things that should not be.

Ever is its cruelty. Ever its damnation bent on ruin.

Selina shivered awake in the dark. Merciless wind howled at the mouth of the cave, bringing the reach of the snowstorm beyond the threshold. The others remained undisturbed as she trembled in the fading grasp of the vision-dream. She'd lived it in sleep every day since being made and no detail had ever changed until now. In its wilting she'd heard a soft whisper. The utterance of a name which had long passed into the everyday language of this kingdom … *Desider.*

He was a scourge of Rome. The Margraviate of Brandenburg was his principality and he the long arm of church rule to its borders and beyond. This she knew. Many were the tales of torture, of whole villages burned in the name of his one, true god. Selina now realised she was being warned, or handed a premonition of her demise. *But what agent brought her this knowing? That which made her or something of a heavenly realm which sought her downfall?* She could not know but was intent on outwitting the wolf on her trail. Given the mania sweeping the lands for centuries, it was no small miracle she and her band had evaded the hunt until now.

It was inevitable that the troupe's activities would eventually attract the attention of unwanted eyes. It brought Selina a moment of clarity and she pondered the possibilities beneath a blanket of thick snow. They could retreat from civilization and survive on animal blood until the life of this witch-hunter was spent. Barring that, a push into far-off lands might keep her brethren from the fires of the holy. A sudden thought flashed through her mind: *for the first time, in all of time, they were the prey.* Now she knew what it was to be hunted. Knew the fear of cornered quarry. She hated its taste—so very different from the wine of humanity.

She'd not return to sleep, instead keeping a vigil over her crew until the storm abated and the moon brought its silver light to the peaks. Stepping outside, she looked back the way they'd come and focused her mind on their pursuer. Projecting across distance, she sought to scan the wilds for an imprint of something human. Only fragments came to mind. The gift was limited but enough to form an impression. They came in number and were mere days behind. Anything of greater significance was tenuous and Selina struggled for a sharper focus, which simply evaded her. This knowledge was enough. For the first time, events in actuality were aligned with a subconscious omen which had dogged her every day of slumber.

What Selina knew of this mortal, and of his men, was a fervent belief in their cause and an unyielding determination to rid their lands of what they deemed unholy terrors. It would be unending, and a war of attrition she'd not have her kin go through. She'd use all of her guile, all of the experience attained over centuries to outwit this adversary. The children of nature were hers to command and she would use them to harry these aggressors, and act as cover in her evasion tactics. The troupe would stay on the move, avoiding direct confrontation but try for a splintering of the pursuing group whenever possible. That way, slowly picking off their number one by one. It was all she could do to stave off disaster.

Later, when the others roused, she told them of the impending threat. As she'd expected, the response from Merivel and Doval was to fight. *If only in their making had their egos been snuffed out,* she thought. A firm 'no' was her response. They stood their ground but she explained this foe was different. By the end, Morpus and Săraca were genuinely afraid and nestled closer on either side of Lillai for comfort. Selina's delivery had had the desired effect, bringing her a measure of comfort in that knowledge. They would trust to her judgement and play the long game in disposing of the menace which threatened their existence.

Hardy campaigners, each man in Desider's company was unfazed by the challenges of the mountains. Equipped for protracted quests, they could survive indefinitely in the wilderness. Each had a particular set of skills which had earned them their place in the witchfinder's entourage. All were battle-hardened from their days in protection of the principality and latterly from the minor conflicts they'd encountered in pursuit of the Devil's own. There was no rank to speak of, only Desider and those at his side in a common goal. They numbered nineteen in total, including their leader, and to date hadn't lost a single soul in any hellish engagement. Though die they would, as martyrs, for their fervour ran deep as channels of their heavenly father's intent.

Valtin, one of the company's two trackers, scanned the ridge contour in the aftermath of the blizzard. Knowing full well the storm would have obliterated any tracks left by their quarry, he instead focused on what possible refuge they may have taken up ahead. He studied the range topography, looking for familiar features which would indicate any possible cave formations. Assigning two points of interest to memory, he waved the group on in their ascent. The ice road presented numerous obstacles and so they chose caution where necessary, but pushed hard on easier tracts to make up ground. They slept little and went by torchlight when dark, despite the added risk of a fatal drop. That their targets were immobile for the hours of daylight was a distinct advantage, though a fact unknown to them at this time.

On the third day out, encamped at dusk for a short spell of rest, the company were handed their first piece of solid evidence. Having taken to the top of a large glacial deposit, Valtin had used the last of the light to survey the upper trail. With spyglass in hand, he caught sight of a horse being led from a shadowy overhang before it disappeared from view mere seconds later. He estimated their foes were no more than half a day ahead of them. Desider was given the news, a revelation which brought a broad smile to his face. Their determination and risk-taking had paid off and he wasn't about to let that effort be for naught. Ordering a lesser rest period, he'd have them press on by torchlight once again and make their decisive move on the morrow.

The night air was crisp and brilliant moonlight emerged to bathe the range in its silver sheen. It would provide a means to pursue at greater speed, for a lot less caution was needed. To Desider, it felt like God's blessing on his endeavour. Though fighting fatigue, his company pressed on, determined to make this span of night the last which stood between them and achieving their goal. Their torchlight, still a necessity for safe passage, was the thing which handed Selina's rearguard an easy sign of impending danger. Merivel, crouched on the edge of an overhang, watched their ascent with a wary eye. Each dot of flame moving below bore the intention of the troupe's demise. He hissed at their pursuers, spat, and then took the news to Selina.

Asked his estimate of the distance between them, Merivel's answer was simply 'hours.' Selina had them haul up while she considered their next move. She read the fear on the younglings' faces and it brought a simmering fury which threatened to boil over. The urge to throw caution to the wind, descend back down the trail and fall upon these wretched mortals, was a rising, bitter bile. But that was instinct, not calculated measures, something she knew would pass in a moment. The key was to keep a level head on her shoulders and put some machinations into play. They were at too high an altitude to bring wolves to their aid. Instead, it would be the denizens of deep caverns which would rally to their plight.

"Doval, Merivel, and Lillai. I want you to push on with the younglings. Barsali, you come with me."

All of them glanced at each other, unsure of her intentions.

"We." She pointed at Barsali. "We're summoning night flyers."

Decades of trust told them not to question her prowess on this. As ordered, the bulk of the troupe, their horses, and supplies, were taken further up the mountain. Selina, having backtracked on the trail with the elder, instructed Barsali to focus his mind on bats in the lower reaches of the range. Together, if their scope was enough, they'd bring together a swarm to plague their pursuers. Atop an outcrop, the pair focused on their primal connection with nocturnal hunters and began a commune. Within minutes, the air began to thicken with their number. From all directions they answered the summoning and converged at a central point before being propelled toward the lower ledge, and the riders who traversed it. At first a dim and distant noise, their shrieks became an overwhelming dirge that swept across the narrow band of rock which held Desider's company.

Ice underfoot, the lesser radiance of moonlight, and the slim pathway, proved a deadly combination in the chaos of an airborne bedevilment. Their horses panicked, torches were dropped, and a fatal dance played out on an unforgiving precipice. The bats swept the rock face in a multitude of passes. Caught in the confusion, some mounts lost their footing as the line got separated. Those at the rear retreated back down the trail, while those out front pressed on at a dangerous pace. For those pinned in the middle it was a drop to their deaths as five of the company toppled over the edge. Two unseated riders fell, while the remaining trio went over horses and all. Of those still standing, the battle for life or death had only just begun.

The screams of the fallen echoed around the steepled rocks, bringing Selina a tinge of satisfaction. Her plan was working, though she knew it would either dent morale or instil a steely determination in those who remained. Desider, at the rear of the now broken line, shouted orders which most could not hear over the noise of the swarm. In a panic, the two riderless horses reared up and kicked at the blur of small bodies which filled the air about them. The rest of Desider's men could do nothing but try to control their mounts, and avoid if they could, the fatal drop mere feet away. Their leader, convinced this was the work of his adversary, cursed at their precarious situation. The loss of men was crushing and he vowed to bring meaning to their deaths.

Separated, the company's two groups took the only course of action open to them. Dismounting and reining their horses, they led the animals away from the centre of the onslaught. Those at the rear did so on Desider's orders, while out front, the rest executed the manoeuvre on instinct alone. Under vampiric command, the bats continued to harry their targets but to a much lesser degree. With the horses moved to wider ground, the fall threat was curtailed and it became clear to Selina and Barsali any continued harassment would be for nothing. But a victory had been won. Desider's company had suffered losses and doubtless vital supplies had gone over the edge with three of the five dead. Selina spliced a smile as she turned to Barsali, who winked in the moon glow as their winged accomplices dispersed into the darkness below.

"It seems the Devil's own are more cunning than we know."

In reference to their sudden loss, Desider addressed the remainder of his company. "Though we mourn our brothers, we cannot stray from our course. And yes, this denies them a proper Christian burial, but our heavenly father sees their deaths in his service and so theirs shall not be a denial of paradise."

The party hung their heads in silence. Inner turmoil spun between his words and a want to honour their fallen comrades. The wilds would eat them down to the bone and it did not sit well with their creed. Desider could read their conflicted emotions and offered but a simple truth.

"If we give time to a true measure of their passing then the enemy will evade us and countless more will be lost in this war with dark forces."

"Having their deaths count for something is how we should honour them," he added.

Once again in a wash of torchlight, they stood in a tight circle at a deeper point of the ledge and pondered Desider's guidance. The thought of losing ground in the hunt and being unable to avenge the deaths of good souls took root fast. The decision to hold a brief, respectful service before pressing on throughout the night was made, and so they offered up sombre prayer on an ill wind. In time, it was hoped, they could return to the pass and recover the remains for burial.

Desider ordered the trackers on ahead, instructing them to bring word back of any sightings made and an estimation of the distance between the company and its quarry. It was becoming clear they'd soon crest the range and by dawn would be making progress down its far flank. Though at first light, the need to rest man and horse would be a necessity. All things considered, Desider was pleased with the amount of ground they'd covered and the promise of the reckoning it brought. In the saddle, wrapped in furs against the bracing altitude, his thoughts drifted to the wife and son he'd once had, and the bitter weave of fate which had taken them from him.

The blaze which robbed him of family, and provided the scars adorning his arms and legs, had been the work of fierce rivals. Younger then, he'd made enough political enemies to bring down wrath upon his household. And the pain of loss always clung to him. His failed rescue attempt, their looks of torment, and the screams which never dimmed with time. Badly wounded, in all ways, he could have gladly joined them in that moment, but would later find God in the aftermath. His faith brought a shawl of comfort. Something to wrap the harm and soothe the troubled soul. Hunting, too, had provided purpose. There had to be a reason to continue and doing the Lord's work filled the emptiness of the burnt-out wreckage within him, though never fully.

The press for morning seemed a long parade of darkness before, at the point of drifting into sleep, the sun's first rays brought a shimmer to the surrounding ice and signalled the end of another leg of the pursuit. Exhausted, and still feeling the loss of their number, the company made camp beneath hastily erected canvases. With the sun up, it was a chance for Valtin to scan the way ahead with his spyglass, though no sign of those they sought presented itself. Later, when rested, they would begin the descent and within a day be below the extremes of high altitude. The day of reckoning inched ever closer and Desider would sleep well in that knowledge.

Chapter 5

Morpus and Săraca

Morpus crouched on a protrusion of rock. Falling snow clung to his small frame, his fingers almost frozen to the bone. Fear had immobilised his thoughts over the past few nights but now another emotion warred within him. And it was this clarity that burned through his veins, because he knew that if the hunting party found them in daylight his family would be eliminated. They were creatures who ruled the darkness, but when the sun rose they were as helpless as newborn babes.

He glanced over his shoulder, and through the blanket of thick flakes, dark figures moved within it, muttered curses filling the freezing air.

The top of the mountain taunted them, only a few hundred feet ahead. Though to reach it they must clear the narrow pathway of fallen rock that lay strewn across it. As vampires they could all clamber over as agile as mountain goats but for their horses it was an impossibility. And without their mounts they'd make slow progress down the other side.

Selina and Barsali's triumph the night before had kindled a surge of hope. *Maybe the hunters would turn back now?*

"These men are driven by religious fever," Selina said, fixing him to the spot with her glacial gaze as though she knew his innermost thoughts.

Behind her Doval cursed and spat on the ground before shouldering another shard of frozen rock. He tossed it to one side, his features pinched tight in the extreme cold.

"They would sooner cut out their own hearts than retreat," Selina continued. "Hate warms their bones."

It was this that rang through Morpus's mind as he focused his instincts through the driving snow. The same emotion curdled in his gut. A shadow at his side as Săraca joined him. He slid an arm around her thin shoulders, her flesh as corpse-cold as his own. She was hungry, but pickings had been sparse the further up the ridge they had travelled, and now this night would be spent clearing away the rock fall.

They could take blood from one of the horses but Selina had forbade them as their mounts were weakened by the treacherous conditions.

Morpus turned, watched the rest of the troupe labouring in the snow.

"Stay here," he said, kissing the top of Săraca's head. "I'll go find us food."

It was a brave statement from a boy who was naturally cautious, but he had to do something. He slid down from the rock before Săraca could reply and was lost into the blanket of white in moments.

There was no track to follow, just an endless sea of snow. Morpus turned his face to the sky, found the cold orb of the moon, nestling just above the pine tops. As vampire he was drawn to her light, drawn to her pale, dispassionate song.

Movement in the frozen undergrowth. He wheeled his attention and focused on what seemed to be a small burrow at the base of a spindly pine. Maybe he wasn't the only one looking for food tonight.

He trudged towards it, the snow knee-deep, each step sapping the strength from an ever-hungry frame. His imagination conjured up a nest of fat mountain hares curled up snugly beneath the ground. Saliva pooled in his mouth and a trickle ran from the side of his lips. It instantly froze. He knelt in the thick snow, began scrabbling at the partially covered hole with numb fingers. His movements became more frantic; now he was elbow-deep in the frozen soil, his fingernails cracked and bleeding. But there was nothing warm waiting for his aching fangs, just an empty space filled with hair and the scent of something that had dug its way out to another exit.

Morpus threw back his head and howled his frustration into the night. Somewhere, in the thick, snow-bound dark a lone wolf answered his call. It made the hair stand up in the nape of his neck.

He thought about Săraca's trusting face, how distressed she would be if he returned empty-handed. He thought about Selina and the scolding he'd receive for wandering off. No, he couldn't go back without something bloody in his hands, so he pressed on down the track, a bitter wind scouring his face as the trees dwindled and he was caught in the full fury of winter's jaws.

Heartbeats came to him on that wind—so many heartbeats that it made his head spin. *The hunting party.*

He shrank against a jutting edge of rock, his stomach clenching with need, his body wracked with the instinct to feed, to survive.

The camp was perhaps a hundred feet below him. The pale shapes of canvas structures were almost invisible against the snow but it was the warm lives within them that drove Morpus on.

"Steady now." A man's gruff voice penetrated the dark, the sound of hooves stamping on the frigid ground.

'What's spooked her?' Another voice.

"Probably mountain lynx, we're high enough up here."

Morpus chewed the edge of his lip. If he could get closer, panic the horses so they scattered it would slow the men down.

All he needed was vampire guile and a whole dose of courage.

Săraca waited on the ledge, her fingers twisting the edges of the woollen shawl around her shoulders. Time passed, time in which she stared into the snow-heavy night and willed Morpus to return.

I should have gone with him.

The thought repeated over and over in her mind. But he'd slipped away so quickly, and now she felt his absence like a missing tooth, a gap where her consciousness probed, searching for the reassuring pocket of his company.

The rest of the troupe toiled with the rockslide, their attention firmly honed on the path beyond it and the freedom it offered.

She made her decision and slid down, following her brother into the wild unknown, her thoughts filled with a nagging fear that something awful might have happened to him. Would she know if it did? They weren't related by the human blood that ran in their veins. They were connected by the blood they drank at each other's sides. And for Săraca this kinship was the strongest.

They were but children in body. They would always be children. It was this that set them apart from the others and this that bonded them.

She made her slow descent through the clusters of pines dotted along the mountain side. The snow wasn't quite as heavy here and the trunks gave her cover, sparse though it was. Her brother's scent reached her and she followed its trail to the base of a pine, and knelt in the snow. He'd been digging here—but there was no prey, no telltale crimson spatters.

A rustle in the undergrowth and she froze, her senses honed to a dagger point. Only her eyes moved within their sockets, her breath held so that even the moisture from her lungs was halted.

Soft paw prints marked the snow, long ears twitched for any kind of danger as a young hare upturned mosses and dug with strong front claws in the icy ground. It was completely oblivious to the hunter close by, that form as still as stone and carrying no discernible scent to the starving herbivore.

It drew level, nibbled at the worn leather of a tattered shoe, and found itself swung upwards by its ears, its back legs pedalling uselessly in the air.

A grin broke on Săraca's lips as she drew it close, the fur soft and warm against her frozen hands. She burrowed her face into the thick down, the heady animal musk causing a rush of adrenaline to surge through her veins.

Her lips drew back on her fangs as she exposed the belly of the hare. She would drink from here, savour the sweet blood that fed the tender organs, hope that Morpus would find her before the creature died. Another sound reached her ears and she hesitated, trying to discern its origins.

Her eyes widened as she spun, her limbs contracted to flee, the source of the sound a note of wild alarm in her mind.

A thud and a burst of blinding pain as she was catapulted backwards, the hare lost from her grip. Her spine met the trunk of the pine tree and this is where she stayed, agony pulsing in time with her heartbeat.

Her vision hazed, but not before she saw a figure making its way through the snow-flecked darkness. A figure carrying a crossbow slung over its shoulder.

The bolt from that crossbow pinned her to the tree, the potent wolfsbane on its tip slowing her heart to the point where her mind could not function.

A man's leather gauntleted fist connected with her jawbone and her head snapped back, pain ricocheting through her skull. Instinct drove her lips back from her fangs.

"Abomination," the man whispered against her ear as his fingers wound into her hair. "You will burn this night and the souls of my brothers will be avenged."

He delved into a pouch hanging from his belt and extracted a pair of metal pincers. He opened the jaws with practised flair, snapping them closed so the thin, metallic sound hung in the frozen air.

Săraca tried to struggle but her limbs were numbed by poison, a poison that would fade but not for a few hours hence.

The man prised her mouth open, knocked the pincers against each fang. She tried to scream as they bit down, tried to scream as her own blood filled her throat, as he twisted the pincers from side to side, loosening the root of each fang. She felt them leave her gum, the cold air rushing in, and a loss so profound washed over her, caving her chest even as she hung on the shaft of the bolt.

He held them up for her to see and she sneered, blood dribbling from her lips. A glob of crimson spittle hit his cheek and he wiped it away with his gauntlet, before sliding his trophies into the pouch.

He palmed another bolt from his quiver, stroking the barbed tip with his thumb, before setting it into his crossbow. 'Just in case you get any ideas about breaking free. I'll bring you down with this one and make sure it pierces your throat.'

Tears burned the back of Săraca's eyes but she refused to let them fall. She was bereft of fang and filled with poison, but her vampire instinct coiled within, nestling in the bed of her fear.

"But just to make sure …"

She watched as the man drew a dagger from a sheath, watched as he plunged it into the snow to freeze its blade.

His eyes never left her face as he knelt and hitched her skirt around her hips. His fingers held her knee and then the blade flashed deadly and a white-hot burst of pain wrenched all the air from her lungs as he sliced through each hamstring in turn.

Her agony didn't deter Valtin as he dragged the girl from the tree, the arrow still lodged in her chest. He tied her ankles, tied her hands behind her back, trussed her like a beast being carted off to slaughter.

Truth be told he hadn't been sure of what she was as he watched from the ridge with his spyglass. He'd been restless and the moon was bright, giving him enough light to scan the land surrounding the camp whilst his companions rested. The wind was in his face so his scent didn't carry, but as he watched he saw the way she became rigid, saw the accelerated movement of her limbs—and he knew what she was before her lips sank into the hare's belly.

His aim was true, as it always was, his bolts already coated in an elixir of wolfsbane and honey.

Witch. Vampire. It mattered not what they called themselves. They were all the Devil's Own and would be purged from this land. Desider would be pleased, but the capture of this abomination would not bring his comrades back to life.

Scarlet blood dotted the snow behind him as he trudged back to the camp with his trophy over his shoulder—and on the wild-torn ridges the sound of a wolf's howl shivered through the night.

It was the sound of that howl that raised Selina's head from her toil. She wiped the snow from her eyes and scanned the blinding blanket of white. Her lips tightened.

"The children," she said. "Go see where they are hiding."

Lillai peeled away, her skirts heavy with snow, her ebony hair plastered to her shoulders. She trudged towards the outcrop of rock, sure she would find Morpus and Săraca sheltering beneath its lee. But even as she slid down and peered into the cleft her heart knew they were not there. It seized in her chest as she raised her gaze to meet Selina's.

Now Selina must make her decision—to continue with removing the rock so they could access the downward pathway at the other side, or hunt for the children. She offered her hand to Lillai and pulled her onto firmer ground.

"We must find them!" Lillai said, even as her feet bade her follow Selina back to the rest of the group. Merivel and Doval had cleared a huge swathe of the pathway, and their onward journey beckoned to them just beyond. But it was still too narrow for their mounts to shoulder through. An overhang of rock gave the vampires slight respite from the heavy snowfall, and it was here Selina gathered them.

"They are wily creatures," Barsali said. "They will go to ground if they find themselves lost." His muscles burned from shifting rocks all through the night and he did not wish to stop until their freedom was in sight. Doval echoed his words but Merivel remained silent.

"What say you, Merivel?" Selina asked.

He tapped his forefinger against his lips, his thumb in the indent under his chin.

"We could split up. Leave the strongest of us here."

It was a suggestion Selina would not like. Their strength was in their unity.

Doval turned his back, wrapping his arms around a large rock beneath the overhang. He began to inch it sideways, grunts accompanying his exertions. Barsali joined him.

Selina made a split-second decision. "You go with Lillai, Merivel, but I want you both back here before dawn breaks the sky. The children will find shelter."

Yet, at the back of her mind, a worry gnawed. The camp was too close for comfort.

Lillai ducked under the overhang to retrieve a stout stick Barsali had whittled. Vampire they might be but any help in navigating the snow-bound terrain was a boon. The sound of small stones rattling made her pause. She glanced up as Merivel dove towards her, as Selina's warning shout echoed through the frozen air.

A moment where Doval turned, his expression one of confusion, before the fear eclipsed it. The overhang of rock shuddered, then split from its mooring. It fell, and the impact of that fall launched a wall of snow into the air.

It sent Selina sprawling, and, for a moment, she was encased in an icy prison. Memories of her making shifted through her bones, but she pushed them away and emerged dusted with ice crystals. She felt her way across to where the overhang had been and found only empty air. The rock lay like a tilting gravestone, the movement of its unmooring creating a cavern beneath the earth.

Her family lay entombed within it.

Morpus huddled by a covered wagon, his plan ashes at his feet. The horses knew what he was and reacted as they would to any predator, with wild-eyed fear and restless movement. One broke free from the line and the sound of its snow-muffled hoofbeats alerted the camp to possible danger.

Men emerged from tents, wolf skins wrapped around their shoulders, cursing the interruption to their rest. Swords were unsheathed and within minutes the camp was on high alert.

Morpus crept under the wagon, his fangs exposed, hunger knifing through him as easily as any blade. His pathway back to his family teemed with hunters, and even if he made it into the forest they would soon pick out a dark shape moving in the snow.

He glanced over his shoulder, felt the harsh wind from the mountain side scouring his face. His only way back lay there, but it would mean clinging to the rock side and edging his way along. Doval had already told him that the mountain was treacherous, that even the goats birthed here didn't clamber along some of the ridges, lest they tumble to their end as the terrain shifted.

The mood of the camp suddenly changed—a euphoria filling the air. Morpus could taste it at the back of his tongue. He edged forward, clinging to the spokes of the wooden wheel, and peered through it. Lines of men blocked his view, and then they turned as one as another man emerged from the largest tent. He surveyed the camp, his gaze slicing through Morpus, and, for an instant, Morpus thought he'd been seen.

On the back of that thought came another. Something was very wrong. The realisation opened an icy fist of dread inside Morpus's gut. The scent of crimson on the wind. Vampire crimson.

The man threw back his head and laughed as another strode towards him with a bundle over his shoulder. The blood in Morpus's veins seemed to slow, even though his heartbeat pounded in his ears. He thrust his fist into his mouth to stop himself from crying out as the bundle was dumped on the hard ground.

Săraca.

She must have followed him.

He watched helplessly as the man from the tent toed her with his boot, watched the grin break on his lips, watched as they embraced. The words whispered were meant for the hunter's ears only but they reached Morpus.

"Tonight we warm our skin and our hearts as she burns, Valtin."

No. No. NO!

Morpus wanted to burst from his hiding place and tear into the throats of every man here, wanted to paint the snow with their blood and leave their ravaged flesh for the wolves. He'd never known such burning anger, such need to kill—such inadequacy.

Already men were gathering wood, felling slender pines, clearing a space in the centre of the camp. He wished with all of his heart for Merivel, for Selina, for any of his family. They would know what to do.

Movement then as Săraca turned her head. Blood dribbled from her mouth, her eyes unfocused, as she concentrated all of her strength on healing her wounds. But her eyes cleared as she found his form. The edges of a smile curled her bloody lips as they formed a single word.

Go.

Morpus didn't know if any other words followed because her figure was eclipsed by two soldiers hauling her upright. They dragged her across to the clearing where a stout pine trunk stood, three more taking turns to hammer it into the frozen ground, fueled by the need to avenge their fallen comrades.

Others stacked bundles of small branches around the base. The camp was a hive of excitement and labour, and it was all to one end.

To burn his sister alive.

Morpus bent over and spat a watery, nauseous slime onto the snow. His gaze tracked east to a stand of tall pines on the shoulder of a mountain ridge. The sky had begun to lighten.

He didn't understand why the others hadn't come looking for them.

Instinct made him shrink back under the cover of the wagon base even as his heart bade him to try and help his sister.

Săraca struggled in the grip of her captors but to no avail. She was weakened by hunger, weakened by blood loss, but still her defanged mouth clamped around a bare wrist and her remaining teeth drew blood. The taste of those few droplets on her tongue drove adrenaline through her veins and she shrugged one of the men away. Freedom beckoned for a few exhilarating seconds and then the man they called Desider hauled her backwards by her hair. His face loomed above her, his eyes as cold as the icicles hanging from the trees.

"What manner of creature are you, devil girl?" His grip tightened. "You crawl amongst God-fearing people, spreading your poison, disrupting God's holy mission."

He dragged her to the stake, bound her against it with iron chains. The links drew bruises from her flesh but she did not cry out even as his fingers fastened the last links around her throat. Her eyes began to water as dawn pressed against the sky. Dread clutched her heart.

Desider stepped back, his mouth curled in a cruel smile of triumph. Behind him, someone approached with a pitch-laced torch, a faltering flame at its tip.

Săraca could not take her gaze from the flame, even as it touched the bundle of firewood below her feet. Grey smoke arose, choking her throat held fast by the chains. It blinded her so she did not see the first flicker of flame as it devoured the thin wispy branches. She tried to drive a fang through her tongue but they were only a memory and this time she cried out, Selina's name on her parched lips.

Through the smoke, countless eyes watched her, but she only needed to see her brother's one last time. Heat seared through the soles of her feet and then the pain began. It crawled along every nerve ending, blooming into agony as flesh melted from her bones as the greedy flames licked around her limbs.

Her neck arched in torment and the smoke cleared for an instant, buffeted by a sudden breeze. Morpus's tear-stained eyes found hers, crimson trails across his cheeks.

Love blossomed in her heart before it was swept away as the first rays of dawn pierced the winter sky. Her skin began to blister but it was not just because of the flames.

Her vision blurred as the blisters crisped, as the internal heat in her body built, layer upon agonising layer.

The glow of sunlight coated her face, taking her sight, the pressure within her skull a raucous cacophony of anguished pain as even now her vampire instinct fought to survive.

The final sound she heard before her brain matter liquefied was Morpus's howl of wretchedness.

She did not see her brother dart from beneath the wagon, or see him bolt blindly for the mountain edge.

She did not see him fall, nor see the men who ran after him peering over the dizzying drop.

Desider watched until the body at the stake was charred bone. He watched it disintegrate and fall into sooty clumps. This foe they faced was not immune to death. He vowed to deliver the wrath of God to every unholy creature who walked the night.

The rockslide was a crushing blow to the troupe's bid for escape. With the younglings missing, and the others now trapped below, fate was dealing Selina some cruel cards. Near frantic, her mind raced with the possibilities. Daybreak was imminent, which brought the urgent need for shelter and their pursuers would also be upon them shortly. What she could not know, however, was that

Desider's men would be backtracking in pursuit of Morpus, he being the bait the witchfinder intended to use against the elder creatures. Selina fought for calm. One act of survival at a time was required. She'd have to hope the younglings could fend for themselves, for if she couldn't free the rest, then none of them would be making it off this mountain.

The answer lay in the horses. With rope, and their strength, the slab could be slid sufficiently to grant exit for the others. She set to work at pace, securing the lengths she needed and binding them to the protruding end of the sheared piece of rock. Affixing the other ends to the horses' tack, she then took them by their reins and encouraged them to haul the dead weight. All those beneath would need was a foot of clearance to crawl free, but as the horses strained against the undertaking, it seemed the sheer mass of the slab was going to deny them that. It only moved a fraction of an inch, with the steeds losing traction as their hooves skidded on frozen ground. Realising the problem, Selina led them to a patch of ground which afforded better footing. Though they still strained and struggled with the weight to shift, it proved a decisive move.

Grinding against the bedrock beneath the rupturing compacted ice, the slab began to move. Slowly at first, but as the horses gained momentum on a better footing, it slid almost two feet before jamming against a sturdy boulder. But it was enough to provide an exit route and one by one the others emerged by teamwork to stand before an elated Selina. Yet there was no time to celebrate. Dawn was fast approaching and they needed to clear the ridge and descend into the shadow cover of the mountain's western slope. It would give them an hour or so in which to find a cave or some other natural cover from the sun's rays.

"What of Morpus and Săraca?" Lillai asked.

Selina looked back down the mountain.

"They know what to do. The eastern flank of this range is going to be awash with sunlight. We cannot risk spending any more time here. We have to hope they lie low and follow on in time by moonlight," Selina replied, sombrely.

The thought of leaving them behind weighed heavy on all, but Selina was right, they simply couldn't risk the chance of losing shelter.

One actual benefit of the landslide was a clearing of the compacted snow which had previously hampered their progress. Now, it was a case of guiding the horses over that slide and then mounting up for the descent. Looking back, they saw the sun's first rays lance across the valley and begin an ascent up the rock face. Spurring their steeds on, they cleared the ridge line and began a careful but hurried push to lower ground on the other side. At the rear, mere minutes into the descent, Selina thought she heard a cry echo in the vast bowl of rock behind them, but couldn't be sure. She merely hoped that what she'd heard was a call of the wild and nothing more.

It wouldn't be long before the sun would be high enough in the sky to pour its destruction upon them. Shouting instruction, Selina commanded Merivel to quicken his pace if possible to get ahead of the group and locate a suitable bolthole. At times, in order to do so, he dismounted and guided his unsteady mount, rather than risk a fall on icy ground. He set a stiff pace despite the risky terrain and was about to abandon all hope of finding shelter when he rounded a bend on the trail and laid eyes upon a frozen waterfall. Tethering his horse to a tree, he clambered down a shallow rock formation which brought him level with the iced-over plunge pool and negotiated a narrow ledge which led behind the solid cascade of water. There was a cave. Cramped, carpeted with moss, and riddled with numerous small frozen pools, but with the horses tied up outside, it would do.

The curtain of solid ice would counter the sun's rays somewhat, but they could also cover themselves with canvas and huddle together in the space provided. It was their only option and Merivel made haste to backtrack and inform the others. It was a fortunate crew who hurried inside as the last of the shadows disappeared from the mountain slope. Thoughts of the younglings accompanied Selina into suspension. It was a dread which made for fitful slumber. In all their time together as a family unit Morpus and Săraca had never had to fend for themselves. Facing a fully grown citizen of a township was one thing, but highly skilled trackers and killers were entirely another. Their way in the world thus far had not prepared them for such a threat. All manner of harm haunted Selina's dreams and a shroud of holy horror settled over her like a deep, disturbing blanket …

Those on fire scream as each tongue of flame strips away their naked skin and mines the deeper tissues beneath. At the stake, they thrash against a judgement which promises no relent until the end. Souls deemed unclean in lands possessed by the machinations of evil. And those their judge, jury, and executioners looked on dispassionately. Theirs a righteous ruin, with all means necessary to purge an age of its bitter harvest.

So much blood flowing freely across cobblestones as cleaver, flail, and morning star break the limbs of spell casters of an unclean alliance. Above the carnage, a symbol of might and dominance perched aloft a tall shaft which casts its long shadow over a hell which professes to be holy.

Her 'children' kneel in prayer. An elder warrior soul stands behind them. He observes. He is their way to God. Opening up their throats with a golden, curved blade, he severs each head with slow, deliberate blows and carries them to the alabaster altar which dominates the interior of a grand cathedral. Cold, white light illuminates their tender monstrous features … frozen in death.

The image of headless undead brought Selina back to waking. The others were untroubled and still, curled up around her, lost in the embrace of rejuvenating sleep. The dreams had been a warning. They'd been a truth. She felt shattered in that cruellest of knowings.

Săraca's passing had been cathartic for Desider's men. It had given meaning to the fall of their comrades. And so, too, was it a beginning, being the first of the deaths they sought to make their holy quest have true meaning. Now they turned their intent on the other youngling who had become separated from the rest. He was at a distinct disadvantage. Daylight had dispatched his counterpart and there was little in the way of hiding places on the pass. Desider's company merely had to hold their position, fan out across the slope, and flush out the other youngling. Though the aim this time was to capture rather than to kill, for Desider planned to use him as bait for the others in the coming days. They'd not seen in which direction Morpus had taken flight, but had heard his distress and so Valtin had quickly set upon his trail.

The wilds were the place the tracker called home. To the young vampire, the alien landscape was nothing but a nameless piece of hostile territory in which his existence hung in the balance. Separated from the others, he was vulnerable, and if he stood any chance of surviving then all he could do was hide. He'd slithered into a recess where a huge slab of rock sat upon three massive boulders. The gap was narrow, too slight to accommodate an adult, but just enough to offer cover for the youngling. The slab itself was roughly forty feet across and set at elevation to one end, having settled as glacial moraine long ago. Currently, Valtin stood upon it, unaware of his quarry beneath as he scanned the surrounding vista for signs of the blood feeder.

"You've gone to ground, little one," Valtin whispered. "I wonder where you're hiding."

The tracker did a sweep atop the slab, slowly turning full circle and looking intensely at the terrain around him. Much of it was scree and boulders, making it difficult to determine the passage of anything much, never mind his prey. He stood deep in thought, trying to fathom what the creature would do to evade capture. Beneath the slab, Morpus knew his hunter had stopped on the rock and his mind was in turmoil. He was sure his bolthole had been compromised. Sure his pursuer was now simply toying with him, and it was just a matter of time before being told he should give up his hiding place and come out. But that moment did not come. Instead, it seemed an eternity the tracker stood aloft and held his position, with Morpus growing ever more frantic before Valtin stepped off the rock and moved on.

In essence, Morpus was trapped here, at least until dusk. Tortured by Săraca's demise, he lay in the crawlspace and wept in remembrance of everything they'd shared down through the ages. It wasn't all death, blood, and carnage. Their lives had been filled with adventure, fun, and the care bestowed upon them by the others. His family was forever changed and there was a very real possibility he'd never see any of them again. It was a sobering moment. Despite his killing prowess, which was considerable, he felt extremely vulnerable separated from their protection. Normally, he'd be sleeping now. The hellish world of daytime would be pushed to the periphery of his experience, being just a minor threat which was always skilfully avoided by Selina's crew. Yet, here he was trapped against the full fury of the sun's rage. At the mercy of mere mortals.

The hours seemed endless. At times, Morpus heard distant voices. At others, the wind brought a multitude of eerie calls to the landscape. He drifted into sleep occasionally, only to be snapped back to wakefulness with the possibility of a threat close by. The range seemed haunted with movement, but all of it far away and seemingly designed to heighten his fear. Undoubtedly, there were sounds of the hunting party in all of it, but there wasn't anything distinct to determine the source. It was a torturous span of solitude. When fingers of shade began to reach long, and with definition, there seemed an ending in sight and the possibility of reuniting with the others. A few more hours would see the onset of nightfall and perhaps safe passage to the other side of the range.

In the half light, a skylark came to ground and tasked itself with extracting a snail from its shell. In calculated strokes, it beat its meal against a rock, breaking away the mollusc's armour piece by piece until all protection was gone. Morpus watched transfixed. The comparison between the bird and the snail, and he and his hunters was all too real. Here, in his rock shell, he was relatively safe, but if he lost that … The lark took flight and with it went the notion of capture. It was easy for basic fears to prey on Morpus's mind. He tried not to allow them to overtake all reason. Darkness was coming, and with it the opportunity to emerge from hiding and clear the ridge into the awaiting valley beyond. His pursuers would soon be reliant on torchlight, meaning he would see them at distance and give them a wide berth in his bid for escape.

Footfalls came suddenly within earshot. A backtracking Valtin stood once again on the slab which shielded his target. It was a crush to hope for Morpus in that moment but he soon realised the tracker was simply retracing his steps, and not ensnaring his prey. Another laboured hour slipped by, bringing with it the veil of night Morpus had desperately craved. Crawling free, he stayed low and crept forward to a cluster of boulders, onto which he tentatively clambered to use as a vantage point to survey the surrounding area. And, as reasoned, torches were indeed the giveaway. Morpus saw their bearers everywhere. Some walked in packs, while others acted alone in their pursuit of him. He was confident he could outwit them and go undetected under the cover of night.

He moved with otherworldly stealth, something his hunters did not. The darkness was his ally and he used it to great advantage. He barely made a sound as he ascended the slope, keeping to natural cover at every turn. Desider's company had worked ceaselessly all day to flush out their quarry. They were tired and frustrated, and had quickly concluded they'd lost their advantage as the chance of a daylight ensnarement had been squandered. They were, however, relentless and driven by an unwavering fervour for the cause. They'd hunt all night and beyond if needed. Desider himself kept his own vigil by the campfire. Safe in the knowledge his men would not fail, he'd taken the day to ponder Săraca's demise and make detailed notes regarding these new specimens of evil. He studied the fangs Valtin had extracted by firelight and detailed them in Latin in the treatise he was compiling.

It seemed plausible these creatures could be widespread. He deemed it unlikely they were merely localised and so made a mental note to consult with scholastic institutes when this pack had been eradicated. By charting his findings, it was his hope this knowledge would aid others in the war against agents of the Devil. He pocketed the teeth and continued his notes. A few of his men returned for some respite and a hot drink, but their intent was to head back out after only a brief return to camp. His warm smile and acknowledgement of their efforts shot them through with renewed purpose. He never doubted their tenacity for a second. Each was a good man, dedicated to holy service. And when later they left the camp, he bid them a blessed departure.

"Go in the grace of God," he said, while making the sign of the cross.

Morpus merely had to trust his instincts and work the cover of night to his advantage in order to elude his would-be captors. His confidence grew with each torchbearer he evaded and his advance along the pass was one of steady progress, which buoyed his hopes of reuniting with Selina and the others. As the tree line began to thin, he saw little in the way of those in pursuit. They kept circling back, concentrating their efforts in the area where Săraca had come to grief, and where her sibling had made himself known to them. Avoiding capture looked a certainty now, but only in those moments of elation before Morpus tripped on something unseen and his world turned upside down, literally.

Now ten feet off the ground, swinging back and forth in the net which had ensnared him, Morpus couldn't help the cry that escaped his lips and alerted Desider's men. He struggled to no avail in the tight bindings of the carefully crafted trap. Arms and legs hung outside of it, while the thick, coarse ropework was pulled taut around his torso by the counterweight on which it relied. In desperation, Morpus began to gnaw at the heavy strands but gagged on their fibres. It was futile, no amount of battling against the snare would see him free before his pursuers would close the distance between them. Săraca's passing flashed before his eyes. He struggled as hard as he could against the net, fear driving the desire to escape the same fate. Torchlight suddenly washed over him and he froze.

"Well, well … ever does the Lord provide," Valtin said, and grinned.

Morpus thrashed in the trap and hissed at the tracker, who pondered whether to simply cut the rope suspending his captive and have him hit the ground hard, or lower the net carefully to spare its cargo. There would be plenty of time for inflicting pain upon the Godless thing at his mercy soon enough. Instead, he cupped a hand to his mouth and shouted to the others in his company, waving his torch, too, to guide the rest to the point of capture.

"We have so many plans for you, child of the dark," the tracker promised.

The youngling fought back tears, knowing full well what fate awaited him. Again, he tried to gnaw at the net but it was too coarse and too thick for his fangs to take apart. Utter despair came over him. Death would soon come and it somehow seemed retribution for all those he'd fed upon for centuries. He was sure they'd kill him the way they'd dealt with Săraca. He'd burn in the fury of the sun, and there'd be nothing Selina and the others could do to stop it. It was something he'd never considered. His vulnerability had always seemed a very distant possibility. The troupe had always guaranteed him protection but their care was far away and lost on the mountain. A lone tear streaked his cheek and Valtin merely grinned at the vampire's sorrow.

"Your elders have abandoned you. Do not cling to hope, darkling. You are forsaken," said Valtin, hammering home the futility of the situation.

There was no answer Morpus could give. He knew this hunter had no reason to lie even if the truth of it was slightly different. The others hadn't in fact come back for him and so that sense of abandonment was very real. A cheer went up from the tracker's comrades arriving on the scene. Their efforts had been rewarded with another ensnarement of evil, and as Valtin lowered the net and its contents to the ground, they congratulated him on his hunting prowess. Desider would be buoyed by the capture. It was key to his evolving strategy.

The mood in the hunters' camp that evening was one of elation. They had their prize and it would undoubtedly bring the rest of those unholy ghouls out of whatever nest they were hiding in. Celebration was a swift affair, with Desider keen to push on over the ridge and put their *bait* to good use. Conditions were still treacherous, with little in the way of respite from the extreme weather. But the crossing was a short haul and within a few hours they were over and descending the trail on the other side. Stopping at a sheer granite cliff that jutted out of the range topography, which had a drop of over a thousand feet, the company dismounted horses on its flat top at Desider's order. He walked, torch in hand, to the very edge of the precipice and hollered into the black expanse below.

"Hell queen. Hear me."

He let those initial words echo through the vastness of the valley before announcing the rest.

"One dark child has already fallen by my hand. The girl. Now, we have the other in chains. Be it on your head whether he perishes in flames or lives on in confinement on holy ground."

He paused again, with the stillness of the dark hiding the raging intensity of those listening below.

"Abandon your flight from this mountain. Stand and face me or I will destroy this darling monster."

"The choice is yours," he added, to finalise his intent.

With that, he strode back to his horse, mounted, and the company continued its descent of the trail. Morpus, in shackles on the back of Valtin's horse, hung his head as thoughts of Selina and the troupe became a swirl of conflicting emotions. The way down was becoming easier, for the snow and ice was made sparse by lower altitude, giving them a more secure footing and the opportunity to up their pace. Desider ordered riders ahead, in the firm belief those elder dark angels would indeed wish a toll of flesh for the death he'd wrought on their own. They were to be vigilant and act as an advance warning party. The company's precious cargo, Morpus, was kept to the rear of their formation. The attack, when it came, as Desider knew it would, would be ferocious and cunning. But the men were prepared, and the presence of the Lord was ever with his foot soldiers.

Having left the cover of the frozen waterfall hours earlier, Selina and the others were currently gathered on the safer slopes of the lower reaches. They'd heard with crystal clarity the witchfinder's proclamation. Their anger seethed inside. And, as it was, shot through with grief for the loss of Săraca. It would be so easy to give into that rage and race back up the mountain to exact revenge, but they'd be so exposed and outnumbered, and facing well-equipped and experienced foes. That it was time to make a stand there was no doubt, but how to do it was the question. Anything they did would compromise the youngling's safety and so a strategy would have to be put in place.

Selina looked around her crew. Their demeanour said it all. They were tired of running. Tired of holding back their prowess and aggression. Yet, she herself was haunted by bad dreams which were a portend of things to come. They spoke of ruin for her kind and she dared not tell the others of their dire translation. Steeling her resolve, the notion of coming to an end on this mountain became a quiet acceptance. *If it came to pass, then so be it.* They discussed all manner of tactics before settling on a plan which would hopefully see the death of all in the hallowed company, and the salvation of their kin. That done, Selina walked away from the others and focused her gaze on the line of torches that were snaking down the slope above.

"I'm going to rip out your heart and eat it in front of your men. And when that's done, they'll suffer in ways you can't even imagine. I'll have their corpses dragged behind our horses, just to show I piss on your God and all that is holy," she vowed, with a whisper.

Chapter 6

The Path to Ruin

Merivel rode hard throughout the night. Sent ahead by Selina, he found the perfect place for their planned ambush. Returning to the others, he brought word that if they pushed on at pace, they could use the remainder of the darkness to get themselves entrenched, and their traps rigged for ruin before sun-up. Along the way, the troupe had been cutting down stout branches, lashing them to saddles, and dragging them behind their steeds. The company's trackers would hopefully assume it a tactic to cover their tracks, when in truth it was for a purpose more suited to pain. Now a good distance along the valley floor, the vampiric riders entered the crumbling boundary walls of a long-abandoned town.

Four decades previously, smallpox had visited its destruction here. Fearing a spread, the local ruling aristocracy had asked for help from the Prussian military. With a unit dispatched, the order was a simple one: containment by any and all means. It handed carte blanche to the commanding officer, who deemed it necessary to nail in all residents and put to the sword any who disobeyed. Though not all were infected, every man, woman, and child became part of a grim statistic. Those free of the pox simply died of starvation as weeks turned into a month of quarantine. And so the town, once a hive of trade, prosperity, and rural charm, was considered cursed, and became a nameless, soulless place.

In an overgrown town square they dismounted and exhausted horses took on water from an old stone trough. The very air there seemed derelict. Death and misfortune clung to the bones of a place they'd never left. Even Selina shivered, despite the line between dying and un-death being her speciality.

"Such a fitting place for a witchfinder's grave," she said.

But there was little time for contemplating the outcome. Daylight would bring its hellfire soon enough, and there was much to prepare in the interim. All the branches they'd collected were taken to the site of a former smithy and had their shafts stripped of the lesser materials. This fell to Lillai and Barsali, while Merivel and Doval searched for suitable ground for the traps, under Selina's guidance.

"We'll dig two pits. Make the depth to groin height. That will be enough."

The pair simply nodded at her command and began digging at the site they'd chosen. Later, with the excavation almost complete, they were joined by Barsali and Lillai who furnished them with numerous sharpened strong timbers and thinner shafts of near-equal length.

"How will we disguise this? Soil won't be enough," Doval asked of Selina.

"We'll put back the overgrowth you've stripped away. His company will need rest after their efforts on the mountain, so I don't think they'll be here until sundown.

Remember, we'll be luring them, so their eyes will be fixed on us, not on the ground," Selina replied.

Understanding fully, Merivel joined the conversation.

"They'll be moving by torchlight, Doval. Bent on injury or capture. The ground needs only to pass a fleeting glance, if any."

Doval scratched his chin. Thought for a second, then offered up his own observation.

"We'll trap four or five at best with these pits. But the panic it will cause should give us time to bloody some of the others."

It seemed the general consensus, for they all nodded and set about completing the task of concealment. The stout spikes that stood vertical were covered by the thinner branches, with the soil and ground foliage used for cover on top. And now satisfied the pits would pass for solid ground given the conditions, and the frantic nature of the moment, they pressed on with their other preparations. Selina took the chance to do what she'd only done a few times in their history together. Trinkets, collected over the centuries, were retrieved from her bag. A set of non-matching silver claw rings were decanted from a silk purse and placed on fingers and thumbs one by one. Normally used to prick victims' wrists for the more leisurely consumption of blood, they made a fabulous set of improvised talons for the ripping out of throats.

Next, she removed a small, curved dagger in an ornate scabbard. She'd acquired it an age ago while feasting on the offspring of Hungarian nobles. It was with this she intended to cut out the witchfinder's heart. Satisfied with her plans, and the devices she'd use, she took the claw rings off and put those, along with the dagger, back in the bag. The turn of the Earth played harbinger for the sun. She felt its intensity, though it had not yet crested the horizon. The others felt it too. Safe in one of the few buildings still standing with its roof intact, they made their communal nest among the horses in a stable, and took their rest in the near pitch black interior.

Desider's company was weary. They'd spent many hours searching for Morpus and pressed on in pursuit of the others. Close to the valley floor, they chose to camp by a stream which fed the river below. Dawn was fast approaching and exhaustion was all. They needed to get their captive under canvas, lest they lose their prize to daylight. While the camp was hastily thrown up, Valtin, seemingly undeterred by the need for sleep, went ahead to scout out the terrain and have signs of passage inform him where their quarry had headed. Satisfied he knew enough to stay on their tail, he returned after sunrise and slept next to the shackled vampire youngling.

It was late afternoon before anyone roused in camp. As always, it was Valtin first, who began preparing a fire for hot food. When Desider emerged he stifled the urge to order a swift exit from camp. His men deserved, and needed, a good feed, and the Lord's work would be better served by those with a full stomach. There'd be a reckoning this day. He felt it in his blood. Making a mental note to find out the name of this piece of territory, he'd ensure in the chronicling of events it was recorded as the place where evil fell under the hammer of God.

"Valtin, how is the creature?" Desider asked.

The tracker stopped mid-mouthful and turned. "He seems weak. Withdrawn and listless. Needing his own food, no doubt," he replied, with a slight shrug.

"Even though it pains me to have to take the life of another of God's creatures, go find him something in the woods when you've eaten. We can't have him at death's door when dangling him as bait for the others."

The tracker nodded at the command and went back to his well-earned meal.

Desider had his portion of the stew brought to his tent, where he barely touched it. He sat contemplating the many souls he and his men had saved from hellfire since he threw down the gauntlet to the Devil all those years ago. A great swathe of Prussia had been purged of its wickedness, and soon the most powerful of those dark agents they'd faced would be given back God's grace. He'd go home then, retire and spend his twilight years tending the garden and reading scripture. By the time Valtin had returned to camp with a hare for Morpus to drain, and the rest of the men had packed away all canvas, it was already dusk. Now in their saddles and ready for the off, Desider addressed them for what he hoped would be the final time.

"I owe each of you much. A debt I can never repay. You have followed without question and never turned from the Lord's work in the face of such unbridled evil. Let us make this fight our last, and return to the mundane and the peaceful, knowing our hearts are blessed and promised to the keeping of the Lord."

"Let us pray," he added.

They bowed their heads, and Morpus, once again in the net on the back of Valtin's horse, scowled at them all. Silently, he hoped Selina and the others would slaughter these worthless men, if indeed they'd not fled and left him at their mercy, as the tracker had teased. Finished with prayer, they departed. The mood was sombre as they rode. Each man was silently making his peace with God, should they fall in the battle to come. Knowing the foe they faced, some reduction to the ranks was deemed inevitable. This near silent procession found the old highway within the hour. A hanging cage at the crossroads, with the remnants of its long-dead occupant, creaked on its suspension hook in the chill wind which had risen.

If it was an omen, it went unrecognised, because faith quelled superstition in these so-called days of enlightenment. The direction the troupe had taken was obvious, even by torchlight to the untrained eye. They followed the drag marks of the felled branches and a handful among them scoffed at what was perceived to be a poor attempt at concealment. The lane they traversed parallelled the river and the water's rush around rocks dominated all sounds in the valley. It spoke to Desider of a ritualistic cleansing, who was comforted by the thought that dark stains were being washed from the land. How apt on this vital crusade.

Odour was the first indicator the way ahead was changing. Sampled first by their horses, it was a smell which embodied historic decay, yet persisted as a dismal atmosphere which clung to its place of origin. A lone branch of fork lightning flared on the far horizon and a distant storm began its requiem ballet. The town's south gate loomed out of the darkness, its towers crumbling either side of where the wooden gate itself had long rotted to nothing. Choked with vines, it seemed nature was either trying to hold the township together or drag it into the doom of its grave. And this gaping fractured maw swallowed a company willing to ride into the lungs of its gloomy interior.

Mounts became skittish, yet on they pressed, but those warnings were noted by Valtin. His gut feeling became a knot of growing anxiety.

"We should dismount," he told Desider.

"Why so?"

"This place … there is so much cover. If we're ambushed the horses might bolt. It will be chaos."

Seeing the rationale, Desider raised a hand and brought the company to a halt. He gave the order to dismount and their steeds were tied to whatever timbers were still standing.

Morpus was freed of the netting, but led by shackles as they made their way, weapons drawn, into the heart of town. An orderly search of each derelict building, either side of the street, was made as they moved double-file along it. Those first over thresholds were covered by others employing crossbows, with the method simply repeated site by site. The storm flickered and rumbled in the distance, a phantom backdrop that a fated hour found hanging over a ghostly scene.

Eventually, they spilt from the street into the town square and fanned out to cast torchlight in all directions. Illuminated enough, the square's layout was revealed and the temptation to splinter the company and investigate all routes at once was a lure, but Desider resisted. Something told him safety in numbers was the order of the day. Besides, the plan was to use the youngling as bait and the broad, strong timbers of the gallows standing there provided the perfect stage on which to act that out. Though choked with nature's creepers, it was still the imposing scaffold it had always been, and still fit for purpose to mete out any necessary punishment.

Morpus was dragged to the structure by Desider himself. A rope was quickly fashioned into a noose by one of his men and rigged aloft. Still in shackles, the youngling was hoisted off his feet with the rope around his neck, which was tied off on a protruding peg. A second rope was wrapped about his ankles and three other men pulled it taut, leaving Morpus suspended mid-air and being stretched by the pressure on spine and feet. He gagged and shook in spasm, the pain unbearable. Desider simply looked through him and shouted his challenge into the night.

"I know you see this. Face me, lest his head come away and be my trophy."

Barsali, Doval, and Merivel had to give serious check to their fury in their place of hiding. Lillai looked away and buried herself in Selina's arms, who held her close and closed her own eyes against the youngling's torture. They could ill afford to stray from their plan, this they knew, but the temptation to rush in was strong. Instead, they had to stand by and do nothing as Morpus was dealt pain the likes of which he'd never endured before.

'I'll wager that slender neck won't take long to crack. The throat burst, and the head sever like a tender medallion on a butcher's block,' Desider said, as he circled the apparatus.

All the while the witchfinder gestured towards his captive, making good use of the spectacle by trying to foster a guilt in those who allowed the suffering to endure. But it didn't have the desired effect and he eventually had the youngling taken down.

"So, you will not yield to such blunt tools of persuasion," Desider shouted into the night.

He strode up the gallows steps, walked across to the young vampire who lay prone and gasping, and squatted down to stroke his hair.

"Then I wonder if my methods need a re-evaluation," he added.

"Stand him up," he ordered the men on the platform.

Merivel reached for the door latch but Selina grabbed his arm, frantically shaking her head to get her silent message across. Morpus wheezed on the gallows, his eyes darting from one ruin to the next in search of his family. His fear of what the witchfinder would now do pushed him into a strangled cry for help. Pleading, he begged for any of them to save him.

"Will you not help me?" he whispered. All his constricted throat would allow.

Selina saw Merivel's jawline tense and she prayed he'd not break cover, no matter the provocation.

Desider looked at his feet momentarily, pondered something, then looked up and delivered a proclamation.

"From blunt to sharp it is."

With that, he unsheathed his sword at speed, turned on his heel, and took the youngling's head from his shoulders. It spun a few full turns before landing on the platform and coming to a halt near the edge. The body took a second to drop, such was the pace with which he removed it.

Devastation was delivered to those in hiding.

Walking over to it and reaching down, Desider picked up Morpus's head by the hair and raised it aloft.

"I have my trophy regardless," he declared.

Shock rippled through the elder vampires. Lillai fell to her knees. Selina merely stood there, mouth agape, while the other three looked at each other in disbelief. Rage rose up and would have exploded, were it not for Selina's intervention. She saw their anger, knew their intent, and stopped the three males from charging into conflict.

"Look at me," she whispered.

"It's what he wants. Divided we die. Together we avenge the younglings," she added.

It very nearly didn't work. Merivel was inches away from bursting from cover and heading straight for Desider's position. What stayed him he did not know, for it wasn't Selina's words of wisdom or any sense his own mind could instil. Yet, stay he did and the troupe made ready their initiative. Leaving from the rear of the building, they took to the alley that linked to the broader lane, which was once a busy artery off the square. Peering along it, Barsali could see the men of Desider's company fanned out, torches in hand. Sprinting across the lane, the vampires headed for the opposite alley and Doval, bringing up the rear, dropped a rusted buckler he'd found onto the cobbles of the main road as planned. The clatter had the desired effect, for the shadows on the walls behind them were the long, stretched forms of men chasing in full flight.

They led their pursuers along a dirt track, now reclaimed by scrub. The distant storm boomed its thunder in the wake of flickering sky-fire to the north. It spoke of a dread to come but none gave heed to its warning. Something stirred in the tall grass which now dominated the ruins but went unseen by Desider's men. The man himself, near the rear of the company, along with Valtin, shouted for caution.

"These creatures are cunning, remember. Expect nothing less."

Selina's band stepped off the track and into the pitch black of an open door. Their pursuers were mere yards behind. The building was a partial collapse with a good portion of its roof intact, and as planned, the vampires fanned out along its back wall, with Selina, Barsali, and Lillai to the right, and Merivel and Doval to the left.

"This is it," Selina whispered.

The first glow of torchlight washed upon the open door, accompanied by the growing sound of footfalls and further illumination. And those leading the charge, if they'd heard Desider's warning, simply chose to advance without thinking. With their blood up, after days and days of giving chase and roaming the frozen mountain range, they now wanted an end to this business. With weapons to hand, they charged into the interior and splintered their number left and right, and played right into the hands of their foes. Both false floor sections collapsed at once and the first half-dozen men fell face first into the deathtraps below.

Their screams, and the pandemonium, brought the rest to a skidding halt. And though tempting, Selina's group didn't stay to bask in the suffering. In accordance with their plan, they dashed from the building via a rear door to ready themselves for the next scenario. Of those impaled in the pits, two had suffered fatal chest trauma, while the other four writhed in agony with their respective leg and shoulder impalements. Stunned, their comrades were torn between aid and pursuit. When Desider reached the threshold, Valtin at his side, he roared his frustration.

"Were you not warned, you fools. Forget the injured, they're in God's hands now. Get after those hellions and keep your wits about you."

With Valtin now out in front, they took the path between the pits and headed out back. A light downpour began to soak the town, and if it were to get heavier, would undoubtedly extinguish their torches. The tracker spat on the ground and swore.

"This is the Devil's work."

"Yet remember what we are dealing with," Desider interjected. "There is a part of them that is very much like any mortal man. They reason as we do. Plot and scheme the same," he added.

Behind him, in a house of pain, the wails of his injured men hammered home that fact.

If indeed the Devil was aiding Selina and her family that night, then it was he who brought the storm in force to the abandoned town. It had been advancing for some time but was now directly over the ruins. The cloudbursts increased in their intensity and the rain began to pound the empty streets. Keeping to what little cover there was, the witchfinder's company tried to shield their torches as best they could. And brought to a standstill by a cautious Valtin many times, they made slow progress in flushing out their quarry. The tracker was sure they were being circled and watched, and not always by the unholy terrors they sought.

There seemed an altogether different danger at their flanks on occasion. As they weaved among the broken warrens, the fleeting glint of eyes here and there told that different story. Valtin was convinced something else was at play here. Gathering under a rotten canopy for a measure of cover, the tracker informed them of his fears.

"We are watched from all sides. There aren't enough in their ranks for that. If they've brought us to others of their kind then we're doomed."

It was a notion they'd not considered until now. The very place was a derelict hive of decay and despair. *Would it not be the perfect lair for more such as they?* It swayed Desider not. Theirs was a holy mission, and as so, the will of God was in everything they did.

"It matters not. Keep only to faith and good tactic, and we'll win this day," he said.

Open flames were now at peril. They needed somewhere with good cover to wait out the heaviest of the rain. Somewhere with limited points of entry which they could defend if necessary. Valtin pointed to the stables, where Selina and the others had holed up the night before. It stood across the square but stuck out as being the ideal shelter, given its good state of repair. Shielding torches once more, they dashed across the open ground. Now inside, they came across the enemy's horses and the clear impressions of where their foes had taken their rest. The intermittent flickers of lightning and peels of thunder unnerved the steeds and a few of the most flighty whinnied in their stalls. The men shook themselves dry a little and Desider peered outside through a crack in the door panels.

There was no sign of their antagonists, though surely they were near. The witchfinder set his mind to luring them out. Now eyeing the interior, he scanned the rafters, the timber stalls, and the decades-old hay which had gone to mulch. Soon, when the storm had passed or abated, they'd have no need of this cover. A wry smile creased his lips.

"All sacrifice in thy name," he whispered.

And so they waited until the worst of the weather had drenched this accursed tomb of a town and emerged to secure the main doors with a stout timber beam. Carrying only half the number of torches now, they shielded what they had left from what was still a constant downpour, though far less heavy.

"You keep to the shadows," Desider shouted. "As you did when I took the boy's head," he added.

Only the low rumble of rolling thunder answered.

But soon, even it was replaced by the frantic sounds of terror emanating from behind the stable doors. A dim glow could be seen through the gaps of the gnarled and knotted timbers, and along the base of the arched double doors. Horses whinnied inside, almost constantly, and the clatter of hooves on wood were the tortured echoes within. Smoke began to rise from every fractured section of stonework and shortly after through dislodged roof tiles. Inside, a blaze was now well underway.

"If you won't face me, then your animals must suffer too," the witchfinder added again.

Desider's men formed a rough circle so that their backs weren't exposed. The man himself stood separate from them. Behind, the blaze was now a near inferno, with the roof and door timbers fully alight. A frantic clatter from within saw the doors buckle outwards. In quick succession they swung back and forth, held in check by the crossbar, which was beginning to bend and crack at its centre. The fire lit up the whole square and its illumination was made even more present when the stable doors finally burst open, and a solitary horse ran clear. It saw all simply stand and stare at the spectacle, for the animal was engulfed in flames. At full flight in its death throes, it sped past them through the square and was the catalyst for the explosion of violence that followed.

Emerging from their concealment, the vampires finally engaged their adversaries head on. Their pace was blistering. They moved with unearthly stealth and were bearing down on Desider's men much like the speed of the stormlight itself. Tossed torches were flickering out on the ground, symbolic perhaps of the lives to be taken by darkness. Selina struck the first blow in the whirl of exchanges. A man, loyal to Desider since their very first campaign together, dropped to his knees. His sword clanged on stony ground, his shield the prop on which he lent, as the gush of blood from his torn-out throat fell with the rain onto the cobbles. He pitched forward slowly, and in that moment the witchfinder locked eyes with his slayer. Selina, standing there with gore on her claw rings, took that split second to pledge an unspoken annihilation with a simple look alone, before a new threat dragged her back to the melee.

She ducked beneath a blade but Barsali was not so agile. It was Valtin's steel which connected with the older vampire's neck. He was spun by the strike, which bit into flesh but did not sever his head. Yet, that fate came all too sudden. Valtin was on top of him as he stumbled and with a sweeping backhand move the tracker added another trophy to Desider's haul. Barely had Barsali's head come away when Desider's right hand man was floored by a punch from an enraged Merivel. The blow lifted Valtin off his feet and rendered him unconscious before he even hit the ground. And when he did so, half a dozen teeth scattered around him. It took him out of the fight but was in no way compensation for the loss of the elder.

Barsali's fall shot fury through the others. Doval, Merivel, and Lillai weaved among the blur of steel, with all vampires hissing and growling their anger at those who'd hunted them down. It was a disquiet laced with revenge and now joined in tone by the wolves Selina had summoned to their aid just hours ago. They slinked out of the ruins, the very presence the tracker had sensed surrounding the company earlier. Desider realised the heightened threat and charged straight for the lead vampire. He clattered into

Selina, shield first, and the connection sent them both stumbling on slick cobblestones. But until the wolf pack could reach their position, the vampires were outnumbered, and it made all the difference in such close combat.

Doval and Lillai fell together, and Merivel took two blades to his torso. Though not crippling wounds in themselves, he found himself impaled and held in check while his counterparts were swamped by a rain of blows. It was all he could do to look on as the hunters dispatched his companions, with their well-versed decapitation techniques. The fight was swift, bloody, and brutal. No time to embrace the shock of demise or the gravity in the loss of centuries of kinship. The situation grave, the remaining pair would surely come to grief. Yet, Merivel raged on. Bringing both arms down on the swords that pinned him, he snapped the blades in half and grabbed his two attackers by the heads, and slammed them together. It instantly concussed one, who dropped to the ground, and stunned the other, who Merivel threw himself upon and tore his face off with his fangs.

Selina righted herself, spun on her heel, and launched herself at Desider. Had those who'd taken care of Lillai and Doval not come to his aid, then their leader would surely have fallen in that moment. He was off-balance, and vulnerable, and their intervention averted his sure demise, as they put themselves between their leader and his assailant. Selina paid for that move with cuts to her forearms and abdomen, and was forced to back away while the witchfinder regained his composure. But the wolves had now entered the fray.

So now it was those of the holy crusade who found themselves outnumbered. But Desider was no fool. He knew the pack made all the difference. Were it not for the fact his party were now the lesser force he would've taken the head of this coven leader, and put her skull pride of place among the relics of a righteous campaign back home. But it was not to be. Ordering the last of his men to fight to the death, he retreated from the square and disappeared into the black of night. Back at the company's horses, he cut their tied reins and scattered all save his own, lest any survivors should follow him at pace. Screaming, Selina poured her hatred into the foes before her and she, Merivel, and the wolves of the forgotten vale, battled to the last in the sodden embers of the storm.

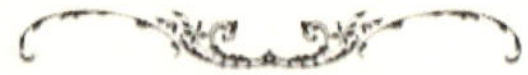

Feeling robbed, cheated, and in despair for the loss of her family, Selina stared at the now conscious Valtin and gritted her teeth. She'd desperately wanted to dine on Desider's heart but that feast was no longer on the menu. The tracker was tied to the gibbet of the gallows, ropes around neck, ankles, and midriff. Two other survivors, stripped of their weapons and armour, were watched by the wounded Merivel. Though he wheezed because of the punctures he'd suffered, he could still undo them in the blink of an eye.

"Your leader has abandoned you to your fate," Selina said.

Valtin, still dazed from the crushing blow he'd taken, tried to focus on her words.

"And since I can't have what I want, I'm going to have to make do with what's left," she added.

The tracker, whose mouth was a ruin, managed a mixture of blood and saliva, which he spat at her face.

She didn't even flinch. Didn't bother to wipe away the offending material. Instead, she reached for her dagger. Unsheathing it, she looked through the mere mortal before her and became lost in thought. So many memories flooded through. The troupe had filled her existence.

Given meaning to what she was, and now it was all in tatters. But that reverie soon drifted away and her focus became pinpoint once more.

"If it's true, I've heard the followers of your god drink his blood. So then, we're not so different, you and I, are we not?" Selina posed.

With that, she plunged the curved blade into the tracker's chest and began to carve her way to the thing she sought. His screams, though short-lived, filled the square and beyond, and the place which had only known dire misery was handed another serving of grim despair. Sprayed with Valtin's blood, Selina buried her hands into his flesh and worked the knife. With the organ now extracted, she turned to Desider's abandoned few and ate the tracker's heart in front of them. Trapped, horrified, and in fear for their own lives, they could only watch as this monster devoured her prize.

"And what of these two?" Merivel asked.

"We'll drain them," she replied between mouthfuls.

"After rest and regeneration you and I shall become the hunters," she added.

Merivel understood. They were going after the man who'd brought about the destruction of their family. Selina wouldn't stop until he was made to suffer.

"You," Merivel said, pointing to one of their captives. "Your leader was the margrave of the north, yes?" The man looked at the ground. Ground he'd soon be dead upon. He made a brief, silent prayer and told them.

They knew Brandenburg was in the north of the country. If they could not catch him heading there, then they'd cross all of Prussia in the hunt and slay him in his bed if necessary. The legendary witchfinder would die famous for some other reason, a vow Selina made before God and the Devil himself.

Chapter 7

After the Carnage

Selina and Merivel dragged the remains of their troupe away from the scene of carnage to the outer perimeters of the town.

Selina took on the brunt of the bloody work until Merivel's wounds began to knit together. Rage bubbled in her chest but within that rage was a numbness borne from grief and guilt. Her plan had been sound and free from the shackles of emotional entanglement—until Morpus's head was cleaved from his body. Bile rose in her throat as she placed the gore-streaked corpse of Lillai onto the ground. A pale arm from the woman she had called sister flopped across the small figure already deposited there. Even in death Lillai protected the youngling.

With their gruesome task completed Merivel stole from the shadows followed by the wolves. They padded after him, heads hung low, muzzles bloodied, the retroreflector of their eyes piercing the darkness.

The alpha of the pack, a large, rangy beast with battle scars notching his ears, broke ranks. He came to Selina and laid his head against her thigh, a growl rumbling in his chest. Selina crouched and took his great head in her hands, smoothing back his fur. His tongue snaked out and licked the blood from her forearms.

Hers was not the only troupe to bear casualties. The bodies of the wolf pack lay slain amongst the men from Desider's entourage.

"I thank you for your sacrifice," she said softly, her eyes meeting the golden gaze from the wolf. "And now I give you what is left of my family. Devour blood and flesh and bone, and take the shadows of their strength."

It was the only gift she had to offer and would mean that the spirit of her family would live on, hunting the wild slopes under the watchful moon as they always had.

Merivel was tight-lipped. His injuries had almost healed but a stunned exhaustion hovered. He drove it back, replaced it by a simmering fury spawned from what had unfolded on this heinous night. The blood he had taken from one of the hapless survivors curdled in his stomach and he contemplated that he hadn't made the man suffer enough as he drank his fill.

"I should have intervened before Morpus was slain," he said as Selina stood and the rest of the wolf pack ambled towards their leader. He spat on the ground and the gob landed at the shoulder of Barsali who always used that act as a mark of his displeasure or of claiming.

"Do you think the outcome would have been any different?" Selina said, her eyes lifting to the sky. Already the stars were dimming as dawn pushed up from the arms of the horizon.

"He would have known that we cared," Merivel snapped. "He died thinking he'd been abandoned."

Merivel's words cut Selina to the quick, and for a moment her eyes mirrored her hurt, but soon they shone with a steely resolve.

"Fate dealt us a cruel hand but I take full responsibility for what happened. If you need to walk away, I won't stop you."

She dealt the ultimatum like she was dealing a hand of cards, swiftly, with no idea what the fallout from the cards would be. Part of her couldn't fault Merivel if he wanted to take his leave.

Merivel gritted his teeth. His fangs ached in his jaw. He knew his thoughts were ruled by anger and grief, and his own inadequacy at being unable to save any of his family.

For centuries they had roamed and been monarchs of the night, and now, in the span of only a few hours, they were decimated. The sigh that fell from his lips came from his very core.

"We belong together, Selina."

The wind stirred and brought with it the scent of ash and burnt flesh from the stables. Selina took his arm and led him towards the barn where they had laid their trap.

"Don't look back," she said as the sound of teeth ripping flesh from bone followed them. "Our kin don't need us now."

Where did dead vampires go? Selina had no use for religion, it made men weak, gave them reasons to commit atrocities all in the name of a deity no one could prove existed. But she had been gutted open tonight and so the thought hovered.

Only Merivel's voice brought her back to the present.

"What now?" Two simple words, heavy with the uncertainty of their future.

"We rest while the sun burns, and then we forsake this place of death," she said quietly.

They entered the barn where only one man remained alive. He lay atop his fallen comrades, a stake puncturing his shoulder. Blood foam bubbled from between his lips, his eyes shining with agony.

"Please," he wheezed through the froth.

Merivel strode across and crouched by the pit. He took hold of the man by his hair and tilted his face upwards. "Please? What does that even mean?" Merivel laughed, and his voice, cold and hard and unforgiving, echoed around the barn like a stone tumbling into a deep well. He bent lower so his face was inches from his prey. "You did all this for God? Let me tell you that he does not exist. But the Devil does and he's saved a place for you in eternal Hell."

With that, Merivel stood and drove the heel of his boot into the man's face, again and again, until all that was left was shattered bone and the shining pink mass of ruptured brain meat.

Selina watched from the shadows. She had found a safe place for them to see out the daylight, a ledge attached to a crumbling staircase that led to the hayloft, beneath which a cavity remained, large enough for two vampire bodies.

"Did that make you feel any better?" she asked as Merivel came to join her. His face was set, his lips a pale, thin line in a face speckled by blood.

"I sent him to his death with his heart full of fear. From this night onward I will do the same for any I discover who think like Desider." Even the name made his guts twist with fury.

"Keep your anger covered with a blanket of guile, Merivel. We will need it all in the coming weeks, months, even years. I do not care how long it takes, we will find him and unleash our full wrath upon him."

She settled on the ground, her bones complaining from the exhaustion of battle. And as Merivel sank down beside her he reached for her hand, their fingers entwining tightly.

No more words were uttered as they waited for sleep to take them, but in two immortal hearts grief rode on the back of each heartbeat, along with the burning flame of revenge.

They awoke to the dull patter of rain seeping through the ruined roof of the barn. At some point whilst they slept the wolves had visited, and now the corpses in the pit bore signs of ripped flesh, a scene created more from the act of mutilation than hunger. The beasts understood the magnitude of Selina and Merivel's loss and had made their marks of unity.

The alpha male stood by the open doors, his breath ghosting against the darkness outside. Golden eyes gleamed below a shaggy brow.

Merivel tilted his head, confusion etched across his face, but Selina knew instantly what the great beast offered.

They followed him, leaving the cursed town behind, moving through the forest with his pale bulk as a beacon in the night. At times he veered off the main track, his nose to the ground, before continuing. He was tracking Desider. This would be his final gift to the vampires for he would not leave the boundaries of the forest he called home.

After a few hours the rain turned to driving sleet, coating the branches of the pines, drifting onto the packed earth pathway that served as the main route north.

The vampires did not speak, both caught in their own thoughts, both flaying themselves over the outcome of the battle. Selina hugged her arms around her body, her jaw set tight, her memories spinning to a better time when Morpus and Săraca would run free in other forests as the cavalcade made its way through. The times when they had a wagon and when they wandered Europe, finding new places to rest awhile and hunt.

She remembered the time in Luxembourg when the midwife had brought the caul from the royal baby's birth. That some saw it as a mark of good fortune battered against her senses. If that were true, and they'd been touched by this blessing, their luck had finally run out.

"Tch." The hissed sound left her lips and Merivel turned his head. What use was it for a vampire to relive the past? Nothing would change that.

Up ahead the wolf paused, looking back over his shoulder. The trees had thinned, darkness smothering the land beyond. He waited until Selina and Merivel reached him, and then bounded into the undergrowth, his task completed.

The track sloped upwards as the terrain climbed and the vampires made haste, both aware that open ground rendered them vulnerable. A cruel wind knifed through the mountains, icing their skin and numbing their limbs but they simply put their heads down like beasts in a storm and continued on. After another hour they finally breached the hilltop and paused to rest on a craggy outcrop, the valley laid out below.

A congregation of tiny lights flickered to their left and the scent of woodsmoke filled their lungs. The chances were high that this was where Desider stopped, but they were not fool enough to hope that he was still there. The man had guile in his blood and was licking his wounds. They knew his destination was Brandenburg but would he go to earth somewhere else first?

Yet one thing the vampires had was time, even though the need for revenge was white hot in their veins.

A small farm lay on the ridge as they trekked towards the village. They stole through its dark-drenched yards, searching for horses, and entered a barn that was in much greater repair than the one they had just left. At the end of the building the smell of ammonia drew them on.

A mangy cat leapt out in front of them, scattering a brood of chickens nestling against a hay bale.

Merivel swore under his breath and then grimaced, his fangs glinting in a patch of moonlight streaming through an open hatch in the roof. He was edgy, his nerves rubbed raw from the previous night.

A restless whinny echoed towards them and on closer inspection they found a dark grey draught horse tethered in a stall. He flattened his ears and rolled his eyes, one hoof beating a staccato on the barn floor.

Merivel took a makeshift bridle from a peg on the wall, and, slapping the grey on the rump, had him bridled in a few seconds. Not quite what they'd been hoping for but enough to get them to the village quicker than their own two feet. He led the grey from the barn and pulled himself onto its broad back, reaching down to haul Selina up behind him.

It was the perfect foil. No one would look twice at two travellers mounted bareback on a farm horse.

The track to the village was narrow and laden with small stones but the grey, quieted by Merivel's touch, navigated the terrain without a trace of nervousness. Soon, the lights from the village grew brighter, timber-framed houses with high-pitched roofs lining the streets. A guard, posted under a flaming beacon, dozed on the ground, their mount passing him unnoticed.

The street led to a market square, voices spilling from an inn at the right-hand side. Merivel wrinkled his nose at the smell of ale and stale sweat, but underneath that ran the metallic scent of warm blood. But they were not here for food. They were here for information.

Selina peeled away into the dark, leaving Merivel to tie up their mount and enter the inn. It was a low-ceilinged room with timber beams, a sooty fireplace taking centre stage opposite the bar. Merivel crossed to an alcove where he could best listen without being observed, his sleight of hand swiping a half-filled tankard from a table where two men were arguing about the merits of flintlock pistols. He settled on a stool and pretended to quaff the ale, his senses spinning around the crowded room.

Desider wasn't here: the stench of that man he would know in an instant.

A snippet of conversation drifted across from another table where a woman was refilling glasses from a huge jug.

"You say what you need to, Otto, but the man paid me up front and left without breaking his fast."

Merivel ambled across, keeping his head down. His clothes were torn and crusted in blood but no one paid him any attention. This is what happens when a country is constantly at war. The abnormal becomes something people just accept.

A small boy came from the kitchen carrying two trenchers filled with stew. So intent was he on not spilling his offerings that he barged into Merivel, and only Merivel's steadying arm stopped the trenchers from crashing to the floor.

The boy's shocked eyes met his, and, for an instant, he saw Morpus reflected there, not the Morpus who had begged them to help him but the Morpus they had stolen from mortality.

Pain clutched at his heart.

"I'm sorry, sir," the boy mumbled.

Merivel lowered his head to croon against the boy's ear. "Do you want to earn a coin?"

A flash of terror across the child's face made Merivel aware that some sexual favour was expected.

"I only need from you your knowledge of a man, nothing more."

He reached into his pocket and drew out a silver four pfennig coin.

The boy hurriedly set the trenchers down before two men and motioned Merivel to follow him through a door set behind a wooden staircase to the upper floor.

Merivel wasted no time in getting to the point. "A man came through here last night, a stranger, dressed in military clothes, perhaps wounded. Did you see him?"

The boy's lips twisted to one side.

"I said did you see him?" Merivel spun the coin deftly between his fingers.

"I didn't speak to him, sir, but my sister, Greta, tends the grates, and she said she heard him muttering in his sleep before dawn broke."

"What of this muttering?" Merivel said, keeping the biting urgency from his tone. This was a frightened lamb and he couldn't afford to act like a wolf.

"It scared her, made her run to the church and ask for God's protection."

At the mention of this deity Merivel stiffened. His arm rested on the wall and the child was cloaked in his shadow.

"The man said 'we killed the blood drinkers, but we opened the gateway to my own hell …'" The boy's words faltered.

"Do you know which way he was heading?"

"No, sir. But he left at dawn's light, and the only way through the valley is north."

Merivel ruffled the boy's hair and placed the coin in his hand. "Do not tell anyone you spoke to me."

And then he was gone, leaving the boy mute with silver in his palm.

Merivel slipped from a rear doorway and found Selina holding two horses. Unlike the grey these were fine-bred mounts, made for travelling fast.

"There is an abandoned convent about ten miles away," she said. "We can stave off the sunlight there."

"He was here," Merivel said as he slipped his foot into a stirrup. "And he knows we are coming."

They urged their mounts into a canter as they left the village boundary, equine limbs racing through the dark, the rhythm of hooves tattooing the ground.

Chapter 8

A Lonely Road

It did not sit well with the man on the black horse that he had abandoned the remains of his company. Guilt gnawed at the edges of his tattered nerves but he forced what was important to the fore. He had decimated the evil that had plagued the land, had inflicted the most triumphant of damages. If he closed his eyes he could still see the youngling's head rolling to a stop, his eyes filled with abject shock.

"If I had stayed I would have been meat for the wolves," he muttered. That was a truth he could not argue with.

But he was not such a fool to think that the blood-drinking queen would not seek revenge. He would need to employ all of his cunning to put her off his tracks. One thing was to his advantage; he could travel in the light of day without the worry of ambush.

Desider reined in his horse atop a craggy ridge. His mount lowered its head and pulled at the sparse grass dotting the edges of the rocky track. He narrowed his eyes and scanned the mountain ranges rolling away on the horizon. Far beyond lay his home.

Weariness laid a hand upon his shoulder and he bowed his head, whispering a prayer to his Holy Father, thanking Him for saving his soul and asking for guidance for the future.

The gospels said that God sent a sign to those who were worthy, and if an angel with fire-drenched wings had alighted in front of Desider and told him God's demands, he would have followed whatever was laid before him.

"I am worthy," he said under his breath, turning in his saddle to face the cruel wind that knifed across the gorge.

A ray of sunlight burst through the bank of dark cloud to his left, misty, golden light spilling from the heavens. A screech came from up above, and as Desider raised his head to gaze at the mighty wingspan of the hawk, a thought pierced him that this was no angel but it *was* a sign. He watched intently as the hawk circled, its head tilted looking for prey, and the sound it uttered seemed to echo only one thing.

Home.

Desider put his heels into his mount, a new burning focus warming his veins. He would return to Brandenburg. He would speak of his triumphs, and mourn his losses. And he would gather to his side new alliances, and return to take the head of the blood-drinking queen.

The slow laborious process of trekking through the vast expanse of Prussia became a never-ending circle of fixing his eyes on a new village, putting his head down for a few hours of precious sleep and to rest his horse, and food that he swallowed but did not taste. He kept a low profile, staying in lowly, flea-ridden inns or ramshackle barns. His clothes became rigid with filth, his beard and hair long and straggly.

His progress was painstakingly slow as he didn't move as the crow flies but instead zigzagged his way through the country, always keeping at the forefront of his mind that he must deter those who followed him, for if they knew his destination they would surely know his route.

On a bitterly cold March afternoon with soft snow fluttering from a white sky, he finally crossed the border between Saxony and Brandenburg. A rare smile broke on his wind-chapped lips as he turned his mount towards the small village nestling in the valley.

Heads turned to watch the stranger riding along the streets. Women sheltered small children behind their skirts and men stood in doorways, weapons resting in their hands.

Desider paid them no heed. His focus was on a simple building up ahead, its slanting roof covered in snow. He dismounted at the door and swept the hair from his face as he entered, one hand on the pommel of his sword although spilling blood here would damn his soul.

He strode along the narrow aisle between rows of rough-hewn pews, his gaze fixed on a simple altar where a single candle burned in a pewter sconce, beside a wooden cross depicting Christ's crucifixion.

Desider fell to his knees, his arms held aloft.

"My Lord," he whispered. "Through Your graciousness I have returned to the land of my fathers."

He reached into his coat and brought forth a trophy he had carried with him since the night of the battle. Slowly, he stood, making the sign of the cross against his face and chest.

"This I show to You as a mark of my eternal devotion. Evil will be vanquished from this world, returning it to Your grace and mercy."

The candle flame stuttered as he withdrew, sending dancing wraiths of shadow across his gaunt face.

The door closed softly behind him as he took his mount and led it towards a tavern, leaving the flame to settle, leaving it to remember the glint from two small fangs.

Weeks turned to long months, but time means nothing to a vampire. Selina and Merivel criss-crossed the mountain ranges and deep valleys of Prussia, sometimes losing track of their prey, but nothing could deter them from their aim.

A revenant's memory is lasting, and both spent many hours deep in their own thoughts, the bloody night from the cursed village a constant carousel of pain.

On this particular night, as the full moon of October rose above the mountain ranges, a chance encounter with another traveller brought them the news they had been waiting for.

They had made camp by a tumbledown cottage. It would provide meagre respite from the elements but their horses were weary and needed to rest.

Merivel sat by the fire he had stoked, whittling a stick with his pocket knife. Flames danced over his face, creating dark hollows under his cheek bones, his hair braided down his back.

Selina had gone into the woods to hunt, and Merivel was grateful for this small expanse of time alone. She had changed since that awful night, becoming more introspective, and although he had asked her many times what it was that bothered her, she would only shrug and turn her cunning eyes upon him. Her demons were many and Merivel had his own. They did not play together.

The sound of metal clinking against metal and the slow plod of hooves on the track brought him back into focus.

His nostrils flared. Under the sharp tang of body odour the scent of warm blood wafted towards him.

The man, for it was a man that came into view, was seated on a mule, the animal weighed down by the vast girth of its rider and a sack fastened around its neck.

'Hullo, fine sir!' the man called. 'Have you a remnant of food you could share with this poor soul?'

He lurched down from the mule, and Merivel swore that the beast almost smiled. The man wore the hand-spun robes of a Franciscan monk, his pale face as round as his portly belly. He lumbered over to the fireside, holding out his hands to the flames.

"Rest your bones," Merivel said, pointing to a flat rock. "My companion is out hunting in the woods. We'd be happy to share"—*your blood on her return*. This latter thought he hid behind a closed-lip smile.

"It is dangerous to hunt alone," the man continued, "especially now when all manner of horrors are spoken aloud." He clasped his pudgy hands to his chest.

Merivel leaned forward with his elbows resting on his knees. "What are these horrors you speak of? My companion and I are not from these parts. We are mere players, searching for a troupe to join." The bitter irony of his words knifed through him like a blade through fresh snow.

"I should not talk of it," the man said, "for it is unholy."

A thud interrupted his words as the mule sank to its knees with a sigh, the sack collapsing on the ground. Something glinted through a worn patch of hessian.

Merivel's focus swept across, and his brow furrowed.

Sweat prickled across the man's brow, despite the chill of the night.

"Mere trinkets I have gathered in my travels. I sell them."

The lie hung heavy between them, the smoke from the fire curling around each syllable.

"It is not for me to judge a fellow traveller," Merivel said, saliva pooling on his tongue. But it was not only blood he craved, this man knew *something*.

He stood, keeping his normal fluid grace in check, crossing to their saddlebags, drawing out a pouch of wine. "Can I offer you this until my companion returns?"

The man took it, almost greedily, as Merivel settled himself by the fire again. He raised his head, his gaze casting into the darkness, where Selina stood, at one with the shadows.

The friar took a gulp of wine, wiping the back of his hand over his mouth. "Your hospitality will be graced with God's favour, my friend. And I tell you this only to warn you."

At the mention of God, Merivel ran his tongue over the tips of his fangs, keeping the gesture hidden from his unexpected guest, who was busy downing another draught of wine.

"I stopped to pray on the outskirts of Brandenburg town. It was a terrible night. You remember the storm?" Without waiting, he continued. "I took shelter as a church is always a place of refuge, positioning myself on a pew hidden behind a pillar. My robe was soaked through but my exhaustion was such that I dozed with my chin on my chest."

Another gulp of wine. The heat from the fire and the rush of alcohol brought a ruddy glow to the man's face, and Merivel had to hone all of his skills not to leap across and sink his fangs into a vein.

"I heard voices and immediately awoke. A group of men stood by the door but they did not see me, or if they did, they did not care. Passionate words reached me, but the content of them made my blood run cold. They were pressing a tall man with a black beard, who did not look like a priest but carried himself like one. One of the other men said he had travelled for weeks to get here, because ..." The friar's voice tailed off and he licked his lips. "Word had come that creatures haunted the night. Creatures that drank human blood."

Merivel waited, allowing his guest to ruminate on his memory, and to finish the pouch of wine.

"They were asking the bearded man for help because they had been told that he had hunted these creatures before. That he had killed them."

Merivel's head snapped up and he met Selina's piercing gaze. He hid the smile that had curled onto his lips with a mock show of horror behind a palm.

"So you see, my friend, it could be dangerous out in the wilds, because beasts hunt in the dark. And I fear it is God's wrath upon us all for turning away from Him."

"This church you speak of. Where is it? I need to make sure we give it a wide berth because even thinking of such things strikes terror into my soul."

Merivel mused that he would have made a fine actor given the look of compassion on the friar's face and his words of warning about its location and how to avoid it.

The friar turned, as Selina slinked from the shadows, his expression one of confusion at seeing a woman. *What kind of man would send a woman out hunting by herself?*

It was his last thought as Merivel launched himself across and sent them both tumbling to the ground. Agony laced through him as his throat and chest were opened, as the tang of wine on his tongue was joined by the taste of his own blood.

His final vision was of the hunter's moon, round and proud and strong, shining through the canopy of trees above him.

There is no God, a woman's voice crooned as his heart slowed. *Only revenge and truth and everlasting blood.*

Selina and Merivel passed under the neoclassical columns of the Brandenburg Gate shortly after midnight the following day. Napoleon I would make the same journey in October 1806 but the vampires did not know this. If they had, the sweet irony of a war leader walking in their footsteps would have put a smile upon their lips. This was their war, their need to vanquish an enemy, to somehow set right the terrible slaughter of their troupe.

Selina had not slept the previous day, her belly full of the friar's blood, her thoughts turned inward. Exhaustion clung to her bones though she hid this fact from Merivel. He was hellbent on what they would do to Desider when they found him, multiple versions of excruciating pain and torment spilling from his lips, but she had already decided the manner of the military man's death.

What she would do when all this was laid to rest tumbled around her mind.

This would be an end in more than one way.

She allowed her thoughts to drift back to the time of her making, to the creature in the glacier. Hundreds of midnights had passed since that time, hundreds of miles had been trodden, hundreds of people had died to give her life.

But with the decimation of her family, her zest for continuing had dwindled. She should have been able to save them. Morpus's demise grated across her bones each time she closed her eyes, together with the loss of Săraca whose end Selina had not witnessed but felt marrow deep. Their deaths were a cruelty that weighed heavy on her shoulders; their human lives cut short so her troupe could move freely through Europe as a family group, their immortal lives severed by sword and flame.

"This is the place."

Merivel's voice pulled her from her reflections. They had negotiated the winding cobblestone streets and now stood before the church, a medieval structure with a flint rock covering and a three-tiered tower.

"He's inside."

After their ceaseless months of travelling and their unwavering determination, this was their reward, but still they both hid in the shadows, letting the anticipation intensify.

Selina did not need Merivel's observation. Desider's scent pulsed from the building and she had to swallow the rise of nausea in her throat.

Her gaze flicked to the sky and from the position of the moon she estimated the time to be late enough not to warrant anyone coming to the church to pray. If they did they would not find God waiting.

The ancient wooden door creaked as they entered and the sound echoed from the stone walls. Flickering light illuminated the darkness, fat wax candles atop tall wooden sconces lining the aisle to the nave. Glittering gold plates and inlaid goblets sat on an altar covered in a white cloth, and above this, on the wall, was a simple wooden cross about twelve feet tall.

Selina's lips curled into a grim smile.

There was no sign of Desider although the stench of him hung in the smoky air.

He would return. This she knew in her core. A gasp of horror fell from Merivel's lips and he surged forwards, his hands sweeping a small glass box edged in silver from the altar. There, for all the world to see was Desider's prize, an icon, not of religious significance, but of his triumph over evil.

Mounted on a velvet cushion were two tiny fangs.

Merivel's fingers curled around the box and the glass shattered under the pressure. Selina's nostrils flared as the heady scent of revenant blood reached her. Her palm lay open for the treasure, and as Merivel carefully placed the only physical trace of Săraca onto her hand, a steady heartbeat spiked across her senses.

She was alone, Merivel blending into the shadows before the door to the vestry closed, flickering candlelight dancing over her pale skin, her auburn hair painted with light.

"You came back for me," a voice said.

At last Desider stood before her.

Chapter 9

Desider and Eloise

Desider had always known that this night may come, although as the months had passed, he had convinced himself that the vile creatures from that night had perished by other hands, or that they had not been able to track him down. But as he gazed into the cold light of her eyes, he realised that this had been a delusion on his part.

He was no longer the man she had faced in that cursed town.

A fall from his horse where the animal had crushed him had left Desider with a slight stoop and constant pain, and a few strands of grey now flecked his hair and beard. He could not run even if he wanted to, and his fiery determination to return and continue his cleansing had been calmed by the presence of his church.

What happened now was God's will.

"Did you think we would forget you? What you did?" Her words travelled across the small space between them, each syllable as sharp as a honed blade.

"The only regret I have is that I did not dispatch you to Hell, too," he said, his chin lifted.

"That was your undoing." She opened her curled fist to show the tiny fangs.

If she was looking for remorse Desider could not tell, but none lived in his soul for that act.

"Selina."

Her brow arched at her name from his lips.

"Yes, I know your name although uttering it feels like a sin. Did you know that the girl creature called for you as the flesh melted from her bones? She died thinking she had been abandoned."

He realised that he was goading her but at this juncture it did not matter. His time on this earth was numbered.

She did not speak and he was suddenly aware of the wind howling around the eaves, of the way molten wax dripped down onto the candle plates.

"She was not abandoned. You, on the other hand, deserted your men. How did it feel to ride off into the night leaving them to their fates? In the end they had no qualms in giving you up to me, but this did not ease them into an easy death. They suffered."

Desider closed his eyes for a moment, his tongue protruding through his lips. This was an act that still plagued him, even though at the time he had made that decision because he was sure his future involved more hunting parties, more culling of the blood drinkers.

A breath of cold air drifted across the back of his neck and gooseflesh prickled his skin. He did not have to turn to know that Selina was not alone.

"Finish me if you must," he said softly. "But I will go to my God willingly, knowing that He loves me."

"Love?" Selina was up in his face, her eyes blazing, her spittle coating his skin. "How can something that does not exist love you?"

The door of the church creaked open, then closed, a chilled gust entering with a young girl, carrying a blanket.

"Papa?" Her voice came to them like a lark's song, filled with the joy of sunlight. "Antoine said to bring you a blanket for it is a cold … oh …" Her words trailed off as her gaze fell upon Selina and Merivel. "I am sorry, I did not know you had guests, I will just leave this here."

The girl was not of his blood although he loved her as such. On returning home he had taken rest at a convent two nights from Brandenburg, the girl in the care of the holy sisters. Such was her sweetness that he was instantly enthralled and when he found her praying for his safety outside his room, a sunbeam through a cloister arch had illuminated her slim frame. It was a sign. He rode from the convent with the girl, safe in the knowledge that God needed him to provide for her.

She placed the rough woven blanket over the back of a pew and turned to go. Her jaw fell open as her pathway was blocked by the fair-haired man she had seen not a moment ago standing by her Papa.

"Papa wishes you to join him," the stranger said, taking her by the elbow and marching her along the aisle. Confusion lined her face, her thoughts grasping for some element of logic.

"Please." The entreaty spilled from her Papa's lips, towards the auburn-haired woman in front of him. "Send this child on her way, she has done nothing wrong."

Fear lodged a stone of dread in her throat. Papa was scared. He was never scared.

"What is your name, child?" said the woman.

"Eloise," the girl said, for she had been taught to be polite, even to strangers, for everyone walks in God's care.

"Such a pretty name," trilled the woman. "I am Selina and this is my travelling companion, Merivel."

The fair-haired man swept a bow, the kind she had seen at pageants from players. There was something strange about him, something in his eyes she did not care for. She wanted to be at home, by the fire, her needlework on her lap, as the wind howled outside.

"Your Papa and I are old friends. We have travelled many miles to be here with him, and now you have graced us with such a delightful presence."

Selina smiled but no warmth filled her eyes.

Terror prickled across Eloise's scalp and she wanted to hide but Merivel took her elbow again and marched her up the steps towards the altar. In one fluid motion he swept the holy plates and goblets aside, and the sound the metal made as it hit the stone floor echoed around the church, resounding from the rafters. Her throat tightened. She wanted to be brave, but something here was very wrong.

"For the love of God, let her go!"

Papa's voice was filled with fear and anger and it was this that made the tears brimming in her eyes spill down her cheeks. In the short months she had been with him she had never seen him display these emotions.

Selina forced her Papa to his knees, his arms pinned behind his back; the sound of a bone breaking and his sudden cry of pain. Eloise could not understand how this was happening. Surely her Papa was stronger than Selina. He stood a good foot in height over her.

Her gaze lifted towards the huge cross, a simple prayer on her lips. God would protect her. Papa had always told her this.

Rough hands on her shoulders, forcing the bodice of her dress down. She tried to struggle but Merivel's grasp was steadfast, one hand holding her firm, the other tearing at her clothing. The chill of the church air against her bare skin made her gasp as he tore away her garments relentlessly until she was standing naked and shivering. Shame doused her, her cheeks flaming, her ripening body on show.

She wanted to look at her Papa but she was too ashamed of her condition.

Merivel swept her into his arms and deposited her onto the white cloth of the altar where holy relics should rest. Before she could try to rise he was upon her, pinning her beneath him. She clawed at his skin, her nails tearing flesh but he did not seem to feel it. He lifted his chin towards Selina and Papa, a grin of malice curling his lips.

Sobs wracked her chest, tears blurring her vision.

She did not see Merivel take the gold crucifix from his pocket, was only barely aware of his hand rising above her chest, before he plunged it between her breasts. The force of the impact shattered her ribcage, sending her body into throes of agony. But her pain was only just beginning.

Merivel's hand grasped firm on the crucifix as he slowly dragged it through her torso, rending skin on its journey, piercing organs, spoiling the firm canvas of her flesh. Blood bubbled from her lips as agony wracked the last minutes of her life.

She waited for Papa to save her.

He did not come.

With her body opened from chest to hip, her purity ruined, she had nothing left to give. The frantic beat of her heart began to slow, as pain became the only constant to hang onto.

Merivel bent down over her, his cold tongue licking her ear.

"How does it feel to be abandoned?" he murmured, before grasping her face between his palms. Her eyelids fluttered but his voice was commanding, and she had always been a girl who obeyed.

Her final vision was one of ultimate terror, as Merivel bared his fangs, as she realised that Papa had lied. He had told her he had vanquished all the creatures of the night, that she had nothing to fear when she awoke screaming in the small hours.

The last breath stuttered from her lungs. She died a broken shell, all of her beliefs splintered beyond repair. She died before her God, who did not send an angel to guide her soul to the light, sacrificed on an altar before Him.

"She died so beautifully, do you not think?" Selina's voice crooned against Desider's ear. His throat was hoarse from screaming, the stout walls of the church devouring his cries and that of his beloved Eloise. He had been prepared to die but he had not been prepared to witness the suffering and anguished death of his daughter.

"Do you understand now?" Selina continued. She grasped a fistful of his hair and yanked his head up. "What it is like to see a child die? How is it worse than dying yourself? This is the gift you gave me and I have now returned it to you."

"Monster," he whispered. "You are a monster."

Selina shook her head as she released him, as Merivel came to her side and dragged Desider away. They stripped the shirt from his body, forcing him to look at the ruined corpse of his daughter as they pushed him to his knees before the blood-soaked cloth of the altar.

"Pray, holy man." Selina hissed as she watched Merivel nimbly climb the wooden cross. He stood atop its crosspiece, one foot on either side, her fanged devil of the night, his form dark against the moonlight-drenched stained-glass window.

They hauled a struggling Desider onto the cross and splayed his arms. She fastened them in place with strips of altar cloth whilst Merivel went in search of more permanent fixtures. Desider hung there, the tendons in his neck corded with pain, his teeth gritted, as Selina surveyed his pitiful figure. Scars adorned his arms, his skin carrying the marks of the kiss of flame. But she had no compassion for him.

Revenge had burned so brightly in her heart, the heat of it a beacon that had driven her to this point and now that it was here innumerable emotions assaulted her senses. Eloise had been a gift, and it was this death that calmed her soul. An eye for an eye the Bible says, or so she had been told, her eyes never gracing those cursed pages.

Her fingers curled around the gold crucifix, the one that had ravaged Eloise, her blood still clinging to the carved detailing, Christ's eyes filled with crimson.

Desider cried out as Merivel hammered roofing nails into his palms, as the vampire dislocated Desider's ankles so he could pound other nails through his feet, pinning him to the cross. Blood dripped down onto Eloise's still form.

When they had finished with him, the two vampires sat on the front pew and watched Desider suffer. Sweat coated his torso as he tried to lift his body up so he could draw breath.

"It is not enough," Merivel muttered, his hands coated in blood. Anger laced his words.

Selina laid her hand on his arm. "We have taken the most precious thing from him. His death is secondary but necessary to avenge those we loved and lost."

Yet still some part of her understood Merivel's upset. She had wanted Desider to fight, to hurl accusations her way which he had begun to do before Eloise arrived. Now she realised that breaking a man, even one like Desider, was only a matter of taking away someone he loved. That loss was the thing that cripples resolve, that finally devours all hope.

They watched until the sky began to lighten in the east and still Desider's breath came in short, anguished gasps.

Selina looked down at the crucifix in her hands, raised herself from the pew and went to stand by the cross.

Desider opened eyes clouded with pain.

"Do you see your God waiting?" Selina said. "Or is there only agony and darkness?"

She already knew the answer to this.

Merivel scoffed behind her.

She leapt onto the altar, her feet astride Eloise's corpse. Her nose wrinkled at the stench of bodily waste flowing down Desider's legs.

Torment laced his face, his expression aged decades by his hours of suffering.

"Monster," he hissed, the word almost too soft for her to hear.

"You think of monsters even at a time like this? Where are your angels?"

These were her final words before she plunged the crucifix into his side, splitting his skin and driving the metal home until it was wedged into place.

Blood sprayed onto her fingers. She brought them to her mouth and licked away the bounty, still warm from the crushed flesh.

She would not stay to see him die as dawn hovered, but die he would before the sun rose fully.

They left by the rear door, stealing across deserted streets until they came to a meadow, bordered by woodland. Into the blessed canopy of protection they stole in silence, the magnitude of the night's deeds thrumming in their veins, digging a hole in the soft earth of the forest floor and covering themselves in rich earth just before the sun's rays spiked through the trees.

The sight that met the boy whose job it was to light the candles was a horror beyond his wildest nightmares. The stench of death was everywhere, and he went to his knees as his gaze beheld Desider's corpse on the cross and the ravaged body of Eloise beneath him on the altar table. His cries brought more people to the door and they all stared in shock and terror at the appalling vision.

There were those amongst them that muttered *vampire* under their breaths before crossing themselves, the few left who knew about Desider's history. Yet they would not utter this word aloud, lest it bring the blood drinkers to their door at the midnight hour.

Many lost their faith in God on that fateful dawn, many more suspending their disbelief of creatures in human form that haunted the night. A victory, perhaps, for the two who slept in the arms of earth-drenched darkness less than a mile away.

Chapter 10

Selina Goes to Ground

Merivel awoke to the heavy embrace of earth. He pushed his way to the surface, inhaling the sweet scent of night, to find Selina standing in a clearing, bathed in a silver wash of moonlight, her arms outstretched to the star-drenched sky. His brow furrowed. There was something different about her tonight. As often happened, they did not speak, both taking minutes to dwell in their own thoughts. There was no remorse tugging at his mind, only a nagging itch that Desider's death had not been enough. Barsali would have reprimanded him, told him he was a fool of the highest order. Dead was dead and the ultimate price to pay.

Merivel pulled at the dried leaves in his hair as he crossed to Selina's side. She turned and fixed him with the kind of stare a human man would have gone to his knees for.

"We must find a place so I can rest."

He tilted his head to one side and before he could answer her chilled fingers came to rest on his lips.

"It is time for me to go to ground, Merivel. The burden of my centuries weighs heavy on my bones. I must rest until the vampire in my blood is ready to rise again."

His scalp tightened as the full enormity of her words settled. It was true that he had heard that vampires sometimes went to ground to renew, that the trials they suffered built layer upon layer until they became a millstone they could no longer carry, but he had never dreamed that it would happen to Selina. She had been his guiding star ever since the night she brought him over to darkness.

For the first time, he would be alone. A flutter of dread closed his throat.

"Come." A single word and she melted into the darkness.

He followed for the last time.

They trekked for hours through the forest, the trees becoming thicker as they walked, the tracks narrower. Occasionally they caught sight of grazing deer, the retroreflector of their eyes shining in the darkness.

Owls hunted, the silent glide of wings ending with a small shriek as flesh was torn from tiny bones. They were far from habitation here.

"Where are we going?" Merivel asked the question he had voiced before, but she did not answer, drawn on by some invisible force only she could attune to.

"There," she said softly, her hand lifted to where the castellated top of a tower peered through a stand of tall pines.

They pushed on through tangles of briars and dense bracken, finally emerging to find what looked like the remains of a castle in miniature, the tower and an archway, stained with moss, the only structures left standing. Through the archway, along stone pathways choked by vegetation, the rest of the castle lay silent and brooding. The forest had forced its way into this man-made structure, heavy boughs breaching walls, hanging over courtyards.

Everywhere the deep scent of green as nature devoured what man had dared to erect here.

"An old hunting lodge," Selina said, in such a matter-of-fact way that Merivel did not even question her knowledge.

She ran her fingers along a crumbling stone wall, bringing them to her lips, before turning back to him. Her gaze drifted from his face, over his shoulder, and then she took his hand and led him through a narrow passageway and down the remains of a weed-strewn staircase. Under another smaller archway and they were back in the forest again, this part completely secluded from view.

Hidden in the trees was a small chapel, its roof still intact, protected from the elements by the tree canopies.

The door stood ajar, as though it was waiting to welcome them in. A shiver of trepidation ran down Merivel's spine as they entered.

Gloom enveloped them, the kind of thick darkness that was instantly comforting. Selina moved freely, her hands touching the walls, the backs of the wooden pews, her head tilted. Merivel wanted to speak, but all he could do was watch in wonder. Last night and Desider might well have been in another lifetime.

There were no shining alms plates or silver chalices, not even a simple crucifix, all items either removed by the owners or by any others that happened to stumble upon this place.

The stained glass in the arched window lay cloaked with shadow, the story told there forever lost to the night.

She took his hand again and led him down the short aisle, veering to the left where another doorway beckoned. More stairs leading down, and, for a moment, Merivel had the craziest thought that he was stepping ever closer to what humans called Hell, even though he did not believe in the existence of God or the Devil.

There, in an underground chamber, was a simple stone tomb crowned by an effigy of a woman, her face covered by a veil, her hands clasped together in prayer.

"Here," Selina said, freeing herself from his grasp. She knelt, running her fingers along the edges of the tomb, her movements becoming ever frantic. "Help me." She lifted her face, beseeched him with her eyes.

The stone lid was never meant to move, placed there by men who never dreamed that creatures with far more strength would discover it. Strength and the grimmest of determinations.

At last the effigy slab lay enough to the side to enable the slim form of a vampire to enter into the void beneath.

"Do not do this." Merivel grabbed her arm, her bracelets jangling in the dark. He was suddenly afraid, not for her, but for himself.

"My Merivel," she said softly, her hands cupping his face. "This is not my death, only an ending to this chapter. I *will* rise again." She kissed him and the finality of it brought tears to his eyes. Through blurred vision he saw her slide into the gap, resting herself upon the lid of the stone coffin.

He swiped at his eyes with the back of his hand, then manoeuvred the lid into place, inch by excruciating inch. When it was done, he knelt by the tomb side and wept.

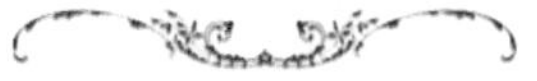

There was no fear in Selina's heart as she closed her eyes, as her body settled into an unconscious state. As she had told Merivel, she was ready for this, exhaustion and trauma driving her into this stone cocoon, where, one night, she would emerge as perhaps not a butterfly, but a moth ready to dance through the night. The world would be a very different place but she would adapt as she always had.

She would survive.

As Merivel pushed his way back through the forest a sound came to him on the breeze, a sound that sent shivers across his skin. The howl of a wolf, a howl that claimed the night, that sang of a life ruled by the wild, ruled by blood.

A crashing through the trees, and a form streaked past him, a great, black beast with paws as big as a lion's, jaws open to show a glint of fang. It disappeared into the darkness but Merivel knew its destination, and despite the heaviness of his heart, a smile touched his lips.

Epilogue

Connor Cohen was well and truly fucking livid. He'd been trekking for days—scratch that—*they'd* been trekking for days, but right now he was so angry with his situation that he'd have preferred to have been alone.

"Fuck. Fuck. FUCK." He screamed the expletives, his voice echoing through the trees, outraged at just about everything.

Luke sat on the remains of a wall, cleaning the lens of a camcorder, as calm as a fucking millpond. This was supposed to be their big break. Subscribers on their once popular YouTube channel had dwindled, as they hadn't managed to capture a sighting for months now. It was true that they could fake it. Connor suspected that's what the other channels did. I mean, how else could you explain the constant appearance of the paranormal in each episode. It's not as if you could book the spooks in advance.

He clasped his hands on top of his head and pulled at his hair in frustration. A ruined castle, his source had said, stuck in the middle of a German forest. It will be perfect.

That part was true, but no one told him about the fucking insects, eating him alive, each bite driving him to distraction. And to add insult to injury, they'd had to camp to get here as it was impossible to drive. Connor hated camping, almost as much as he hated bugs. He slapped at his neck, felt one squish under his fingers and grimaced.

"Can we fake it?" he asked, turning to Luke. "Take some footage, then play around with it when we get back?"

Luke's mouth twisted to one side. "We said we'd never do that, remember? And anyway, pre-recorded stuff is so old school. Subscribers want live, man."

Ever since Luke had hooked up with a guy from California who looked like he belonged in a hippie commune, *man* was the term he addressed Connor as.

Connor gritted his teeth. But what Luke said was true. Pre-recorded was dead. But they had to try.

"Okay, just follow me around, and I'll make like I've heard something." Maybe, just maybe, they could salvage *something* from this godforsaken place.

"What's that?" Luke spun, his gaze fixed on the trees, his eyes wide.

"Very fucking funny," Connor said, slow handclapping. "I'm not the one you have to convince."

"No, I mean it. I saw something. An animal, I think."

This time Connor turned to look. Luke wasn't that good an actor and his face had gone the colour of milk.

"There's nothing …" His voice trailed off as movement caught his eye. "Fuuuuck." His mouth ran dry. It was possible he was hallucinating …

A low growl came to them then, something that made their balls shrivel.

"Wolf," Luke said, his voice an octave higher than normal.

They'd been told there were no wolves here, not anymore, and Connor had expected to run into nothing bigger than a wildcat or a fox.

Did wolves eat people? Connor had no desire to find out.

"Grab the bag," he hissed, "and back away slowly. Don't show it that we're scared." Which was ridiculous as they both were literally quaking.

The wolf advanced, its head lowered, each huge foot carefully placed as it fixed them in its sight.

It seemed to take an age to reach a narrow passageway which they shuffled through. Connor risked a look over his shoulder and saw a staircase leading down. That might take them to a room where they could hold out and hope the wolf lost interest. Jesus Christ he was going to kill Ameen with his smug Pub Quiz certainty. Just why had Connor believed him? Ameen was an estate agent, not David Attenborough.

They sprinted down the stairs, stumbling in the gloom. Fear drove them forwards through an archway and back into the forest, both of them trying not to imagine how it felt when a wolf tore flesh from bone.

When Connor saw the chapel, he *did* think he was hallucinating, and it was only Luke pushing past him and slamming through the door that made him run. They stood in the darkness, their hearts ramming against their ribcages, the stout door closed firmly behind them.

"Sweet fuck." Connor slid boneless to the floor. He watched as Luke doubled over and threw up.

"Pity we didn't get *that* footage," he said, a grim smile on his lips. But right now, he couldn't give a damn about footage, or channels, or monetisation. He just wanted to be at home, curled up on the sofa with his dog, watching reruns of *Ghosthunters*.

But now they were stuck here, at least until dawn, because there was no way they were even trying to see if the wolf had wandered off.

"Just look at this place," Luke said. "No one's been here for like … forever." Awe laced his words, and it was this that motivated Connor to stand and dust himself off. Might as well explore and try and get something out of this damn trip.

Luke settled the camcorder on his shoulder. It had an attached microphone and night vision, a state-of-the-art piece they'd invested in right at the beginning to save hefting other equipment around.

Connor took a long draught of water from the bottle in the bag and set himself up in the centre of the aisle. It was easy to fall into the relaxed pattern of speech he'd honed in the last eighteen months, adding just the right amount of uncertainty as Luke followed him around the chapel. He made great use of the fact that they were probably the first people to see inside for centuries. Sure, it wasn't live, but it was different. And it might just work.

When he came to a doorway, he paused, waiting for Luke to check the recording and give him the nod to continue. Down another set of stairs. He banged his head on an overhang of rock and swore, but Luke gave him a thumbs up.

He didn't expect to find a tomb. He didn't expect one edge of it to be slightly open.

"And here we have a tomb of an unknown woman," he continued, looking straight into the camera. "Maybe she was someone's wife or mother. Maybe someone important but there's no visible inscription." He knelt down in the same spot Merivel had more than three centuries ago, as Luke focused in on the edges of the tomb.

Luke set the camera on the ground. "So, what if there's something in there. Like a necklace or other jewellery. Didn't people get buried in finery back then?"

It was possible, but the longer Connor knelt in that spot the longer a kind of black dread was curling through his gut. They shouldn't be here. He could feel it, the wrongness of it with every breath that he took.

The gap between the tomb lid and the edge was filled with the kind of inky blackness found in the depths of the ocean. And now that he was here, he could smell something, something he couldn't name that was both sweet but rotting.

A sound then, from within the tomb, a jangling that they both heard.

"Fuck," Luke said, backing away towards the door.

Connor wanted to follow but he was rooted to the spot, his every sense tuned into whatever the fuck it was that he'd heard.

A scream then from Luke as from the shadows the great wolf leapt. His body hit the ground and his head bounced on the stone floor, instantly cracking his skull.

Connor skittered back against the tomb, his hands splayed out in front of him as though this feeble gesture could keep the wolf away.

He watched in absolute mute horror as the wolf clamped its jaws around Luke's throat, its fangs turning crimson as it tore away flesh, exposing a column of windpipe. Luke's legs spasmed once, then twice, and then he was still as the wolf began to feast on his chest, tearing away his jacket to consume the warm meat beneath.

Connor cried silently, hoping that if he stayed still the wolf would eat its fill and go away. His brain refused to identify the ravaged corpse in front of him as Luke.

The sound came again from the tomb and his bladder let go, soaking his jeans with urine.

Another sound.

Stone scraping against stone.

He glanced up, saw the lid jerk slowly to the side, dust sprinkling his face.

This isn't happening, a small voice insisted. *Ghosts aren't real.*

He squeezed his eyes shut, felt the dust coat his lashes.

The jangle of what sounded like … .bracelets?

His eyes flew open. The wolf stood before him. He could smell Luke's blood on its breath, a ribbon of flesh dangling from its jaw. And then it did something that sent his mind spiralling towards insanity. It lay down on the floor with its head on its paws like a big dog.

It wasn't really a surprise when a hand tangled in his hair, when nails raked across his scalp and yanked him from the floor. A moment where he saw Luke's ruined body lying in a pool of blood and then he was dragged over the rim of the tomb, his body tumbling onto what looked like a skeleton covered in withered flesh. But this skeleton was moving, its hands grasping his throat, its head rising, its jaws opening.

Fangs. It had fucking fangs.

He'd been looking for ghosts, for remains of the past tethered to the earth, but what he'd found was something far more terrifying … the fangs sunk into his neck and the blood draw from his body was swift and merciless. Veins collapsed, his organs failing as his sight blurred, as somehow the corpse holding him became … beautiful.

His heart began to slow. Her grip relaxed. He felt himself lifted as she pushed him aside, as she climbed from the tomb, her dusty skirts rustling.

"Ssh," she said softly, holding one finger to her lips.

It was the last sound he ever heard.

Selina Dragavei stole into the depths of the forest with the wolf by her side. It was not the same wolf from the night of her entombment but one of its bloodline, all instinctively protecting her as she slept.

Her breathing settled into an easy rhythm as the fresh blood gave vigour to her steps. She would need to feed again soon. She would need many victims until she was fully renewed.

A new chapter.

A new century.

She was ready.

ACKNOWLEDGEMENTS

Heather and Steve (BGP), Mickey (Creative Edge) my community people on socials, friends, and family. Jen, for putting up with me! Steve specifically for the edits, Steph for the formatting, and Daniella for the cover. Beverley for coming on this writing journey with me. It's been a blast and we 'gothed' the hell out of this!

Keith Anthony Baird

For Heather and Steve for believing in this story, Daniella for a magnificent cover and for Steph for the eagle eye on edits and formatting. For Keith, whose initial idea this was, and for being willing to run this alongside all my other projects. We let this one go exactly where it wanted to, and boy, did it deliver!

Beverley Lee

About the Authors

Keith Anthony Baird began writing dark fiction in 2016 as a self-published author. After five years of releasing titles via Amazon and Audible he switched his focus to the traditional publishing route.

His titles via Brigids Gate Press LLC are the dark fantasy novella *In the Grimdark Strands of the Spinneret* (published in 2022), his dystopian novella *SIN:THETICA* (2024) and *A Light of Little Radiance*, co-authored with fellow Brit Beverley Lee (2024). He is currently writing an alien invasion/post-apocalyptic novel called *WIND RUST* which will be the first of a planned trilogy.

He lives in Cumbria, United Kingdom, on the edge of the Lake District National Park and can be found on Twitter/X and Instagram via the handle @kabauthor

Beverley Lee is a bestselling dark fiction author who lives close to the dreaming spires of Oxford, England. Her work specialises in atmospheric horror, creeping dread, and broken boys - sometimes altogether - but are always filled with heart and the tenuous threads of relationships pushed to the brink. All the Feels all the time. Vampires are her first love and occasionally they stop whispering long enough for her to write other books. When she's not writing you'll find her rambling through the countryside, dreaming about male vampires kissing, and exploring time-worn graveyards.

Visit beverleylee.com for more information about her books.

MORE FROM BRIGIDS GATE PRESS

THIS COLD NIGHT

Erica Schaef

Following the death of a loved one, Rachelle Collins visits Ferguson Estate, an expansive country mansion which holds many fond memories, and one sinister secret, within its walls. Throughout the course of a single, terrifying night, Rachelle must confront horrors, both psychological and tangible, to prove just how far she is willing to go to keep her family together.

THE FIVE TURNS OF THE WHEEL

Stephanie Ellis

Welcome to the Weald. The Five Turns of the Wheel has begun. With each Turn, blood will be spilled, and sacrifices will be made. Pacts will be made…and broken. Will you join the Dance?

In the Weald, the time has come for the Five Turns of the Wheel. Tommy, Betty and Fiddler, the sons of Hweol, Lord of Umbra, have arrived to oversee the sacred rituals… rituals brimming with sacrifice and dripping with blood.

Megan Wheelborn, daughter of Tommy, hatches a desperate plan to free the people of the Weald from the bloody and cruel grip of Umbra, and put an end to its murderous rituals. But success will require sacrifice and blood as well. Will Megan be able to pay the price?

ENTER THE DARKNESS

Sarah Budd

During the Spring Solstice, four people enter the caves underneath London.

Garth: a shy young man, who seeks to save the girl of his dreams.

Cassie: a beautiful young woman, who seeks to use the dark magic of the caves for her own purposes.

Bill: an older man with a terrible secret, who seeks to find Garth and Cassie before it's too late.

Sienna: a con artist with a dark past, who seeks to escape her fate as a chosen sacrifice.

Four people enter. Each of them must battle their personal demons before facing the White Lady, who rises each year during the Spring Solstice with a hunger for human flesh.

Only one of them will survive.

Country Roads

Colin Leonard

Something is outside; in the fields, by the ditches, on the roads. Something old and cruel and vicious.

When Luke Sheridan moves out of Dublin city to rural Kilcross with his wife and baby, he imagines the worst part will be his extended commute to work. They can look forward to enjoying the countryside and being part of a small community. After all, his old friend Declan Maguire lives in the house next door and is a Garda in the nearest town.

But Declan's devilish attitude towards drink, drugs and women means trouble is never far from his door. And worse, gruesome murders and the appearance of sinister figures at night mean the countryside is becoming a very dangerous place to live.

Country Roads—don't go outside alone.

Visit our website at: www.brigidsgatepress.com